The Flame

Also from Christopher Rice

Acknowledgments from the Author

I can't thank M.J. Rose and Liz Berry enough for giving me the chance to try my hand at a new genre and for putting together this incredibly exciting new project. I'm also profoundly grateful for Jillian Stein, the amazing social media director for 1,001 DARK NIGHTS. Thanks to these ladies, this is probably the most fun I've ever had outlining, promoting, writing and copyediting a book. Kami Garcia and Delinah Blake Hurwitz gave me some really insightful reads. Thanks also goes to Benjamin Scuglia for additional proofreading and copyediting

I wouldn't be able to work on so many different writing projects while also producing (and co-hosting) a weekly internet radio show without the amazing staff of The Dinner Party Show. A big thank you to my best friend, producing partner and co-host Eric Shaw Quinn as well as our amazing support staff: Brandon Griffith, Brett Churnin, Cathy Dipierro and Benjamin Scuglia (again). If you haven't listened to The Dinner Party Show yet, give us a try. Our goal is to make you laugh until wine comes out of your nose. Even if you're not drinking wine! We're always on at www.TheDinnerPartyShow.com.

Last but not least, one of the highlights of this foray into erotic romance came when Lexi Blake wrote to tell me she was so moved by the first draft of THE FLAME she wanted to include an excerpt from it in her latest novel. This kind of generosity is rare among authors in other genres and I'm still bowled over by it, to be frank. Thanks, Lexi. Thanks for embracing the complexity of Andrew, Shane and Cassidy so warmly and with such acceptance.

Sign up for the 1001 Dark Nights Newsletter
and be entered to win a Tiffany Key necklace.

There's a contest every month!

Go to www.DarkNights.com to subscribe.

**As a bonus, all subscribers can download
FIVE FREE exclusive books.**
!

One Thousand and One Dark Nights

Once upon a time, in the future...

*I was a student fascinated with stories and learning.
I studied philosophy, poetry, history, the occult, and
the art and science of love and magic. I had a vast
library at my father's home and collected thousands
of volumes of fantastic tales.*

*I learned all about ancient races and bygone
times. About myths and legends and dreams of all
people through the millennium. And the more I read
the stronger my imagination grew until I discovered
that I was able to travel into the stories... to actually
become part of them.*

*I wish I could say that I listened to my teacher
and respected my gift, as I ought to have. If I had, I
would not be telling you this tale now.
But I was foolhardy and confused, showing off
with bravery.*

*One afternoon, curious about the myth of the
Arabian Nights, I traveled back to ancient Persia to
see for myself if it was true that every day Shahryar
(Persian: شهریار, "king") married a new virgin, and then
sent yesterday's wife to be beheaded. It was written
and I had read, that by the time he met Scheherazade,
the vizier's daughter, he'd killed one thousand
women.*

*Something went wrong with my efforts. I arrived
in the midst of the story and somehow exchanged
places with Scheherazade – a phenomena that had
never occurred before and that still to this day, I
cannot explain.*

*Now I am trapped in that ancient past. I have
taken on Scheherazade's life and the only way I can
protect myself and stay alive is to do what she did to
protect herself and stay alive.*

*Every night the King calls for me and listens as I spin tales.
And when the evening ends and dawn breaks, I stop at a
point that leaves him breathless and yearning for more.
And so the King spares my life for one more day, so that
he might hear the rest of my dark tale.*

*As soon as I finish a story... I begin a new
one... like the one that you, dear reader, have before
you now.*

1

CASSIDY

The first sheets of rain pound the parked cars and filigree ironwork all around her with enough power to give off spray, forcing Cassidy Burke to hurry for the cover of the nearest balcony.

When she starts to run, the giant rolls of tapestry in her arms slide back and forth, giving her no choice but to launch into what her best friend Shane would probably call "a *Cirque du Soleil* move," a desperate sideways and backward dance intended to keep the whole precarious assemblage of outstretched arms, toile-patterned fabrics, and slippery plastic coverings from slamming to the wet sidewalk.

It works, thank God; her balance is back, and just in time. No such luck with her bangs. When she puckers her bottom lip and tries to blow them out of her eyes, they remain sealed to her forehead, her hair soaked to its roots.

For several days now the French Quarter has been in a drowsy, post-Mardi Gras slump, but the heavy downpour sends it into a coma. She's the only pedestrian in sight, which makes her feel like the only human east of Canal Street. And now she's trapped, all because some silly vendor scheduled his delivery for the week before when she'd told him specifically the shop would be closed. But it's not Leonard DeVille's fault she walked to the UPS store without an umbrella or a raincoat. Still, parking is a nightmare on these narrow streets, laid as they were in the age of horse-drawn carriages, and she knew she'd need both arms free to carry the shipment back to the little gift shop she's owned for two years.

Two-and-a-half-years, she reminds herself, keenly aware, once again, that ever since she became a business owner she's tended to round down her every accomplishment, as if no achievement of hers will be good enough until Cassidy's Corner is out of the red and fulfilling Internet orders from all over the world. *Then* everything will be better; *then* she will earn the respect of her husband's fellow architects at Chaisson & Landry, men and women who currently see her as nothing more than a housewife with a love of long novels and a codependent friendship with her gay best friend. And *then* she will never have another insecurity in the world. Ever.

If she's not careful, this cruel, self-defeating line of thought will wash away her ambitions with the speed and ease of the rain sluicing through the gutters overhead.

She's not a teenager anymore. She has no business blaming others for the terrible pressure she places on herself at the start of every workday. And if she doesn't watch herself, she'll make it Andrew's fault, too. If he weren't so driven and successful, she wouldn't feel the need to compete. And if he weren't so goddamn handsome, then she wouldn't constantly feel like she didn't deserve him, that other women were whispering things behind her back, things like, "What'd she do to land that one? Does it involve splits?"

It is fear that tricks her into seeing the blessings in her life as obstacles. It is fear, plain and simple, that twines its black fingers through the love and respect she has for her husband, pulling it apart until its strands look like chains. And nothing good in her life has ever come from treating fear like a teacher.

Worse, these thoughts are just painful distractions from uncomfortable, everyday realities. Owning a business is a lot harder than she thought it would be. That's the long and short of it. And it's just easier to indulge paranoid fantasies than it is to balance the books, conduct bi-weekly inventories, and stay abreast of trade conventions where she might find that rare, expensive specialty item that will snag the attention of a tourist from Atlanta or a Garden District housewife wandering the Quarter after brunch at Galatoire's.

And then there's what happened during Mardi Gras.

Cassidy screws her eyes shut to keep the memory at bay. For a split second, she worries the effort might launch her from her body, causing her to drop the rolls of tapestry after all. To anyone peering at her through a nearby window she probably looks like she's suffering from a crippling phobia of rain, what with her furrowed brow and her rapid, shallow breaths lifting her soaked blouse. How could they possibly know she's trying not to feel the dizzying, seductive caress of her husband's breath against one side of her neck and her best friend's lips against the other?

Stop it. Everything's fine. Stranger things have happened during Mardi Gras. You're lucky it wasn't— She's at a loss for how to finish this thought. Worse? Better? Are they one and the same when you find yourself on the verge of surrendering to a threesome with your husband and your best friend?

When the smell hits her, she assumes she's having a stroke. Isn't that how it works? Burnt toast. That's what people report smelling in the moment before an artery gives way or one side of their body goes limp.

But while there is a light, toasty quality to the aroma filling her nostrils, it's more like a top note, and the smells beneath it are multiplying. In her mind's eye, she sees the petals of a blossom falling away and wonders if that's exactly what's happening; if the rain has pummeled a potted flower somewhere nearby with enough strength to peel it apart until its central bud is unleashing raw, earthy scents that are blending with the oil in the gutters. But there are no planters nearby, not on the window ledges or front steps in either direction. Maybe on the balcony overhead...? No, that's probably not right either. These smells are not of the earth. These smells are...*men.*

She cackles at the thought. Ridiculous! But it's there. And not just any men either—*her* men.

Her men? Insane to think of them in that way! Her husband, maybe. But not Shane. Not proud, gay Shane, with his endless series of casual boyfriends. It doesn't matter. Whatever title she bestows upon them, their combined essences have somehow joined her on this tiny island of dry sidewalk amidst the storm.

Here is her husband's familiar musk, tempered by a sweeter scent that reminds her of baking bread. It makes her see the dark rings around his nipples and the smooth sweep of his tan, muscular inner thigh where she loves to rest her hand after sex. Then another, less familiar set of aromas intrudes, a lighter bouquet she was accustomed to smelling from a safe distance until a few nights before. Shane is sweet olive with a hint of earthy vetiver, both of which make her see his blue eyes and the gentle angel's press in his upper lip, the startled expression he gave her after their thrilling and forbidden kiss. A kiss he gave her, in part, because her husband put his hand on the back of his neck and made him do it.

How could her efforts have backfired so badly? She tried to dispel the shocking memory of their—she wants to call it a *mistake* again, but the overpowering smells haven't waned and for some reason they make it impossible for her to hold fast to the judgment-filled word.

In her effort to forget that night—not a night really, just a few minutes before they were interrupted—she has summoned the smells of it. The smell of them. *Together*. What other explanation could there be?

The wood plank sign hanging above the entrance to the courtyard across the street is brand-new, Cassidy is sure of it. It looks weathered and old but so do the signs for most of the shops in the Quarter, and often because they've been treated to look that way. She has to squint to make out the logo, a vague outline of something that's been carved into the wood and painted gold. A flame, a tiny candle's flame, and beneath it the words, *Feu de Coeur*. She has only a few years of high school French behind her, but she thinks it means *fire of the heart*.

For a few seconds, she's convinced the sign is another piece of some elaborate hallucination. But the tiny gold flame and the store's prim French name can only mean one thing—a candle shop. And thank God, because it's an explanation. She's not having a stroke or some out-of-body experience. And she's not suffering from madness induced by almost taking an insane sexual risk with the two men she loves the most.

It's a candle shop. That's what she smells.

The rain has lessened, but not enough to justify walking across the street toward the courtyard's entrance without fear of damaging the tapestries in her arms. Still, she won't be convinced she's not crazy or delirious until she sets foot inside the shop itself.

The courtyard is home to a tiny coffee shop, a gurgling fountain, and riots of banana trees erupting from dirt squares that reveal what fragile cover the brick floor underfoot gives to the wet soil. At first, Cassidy thinks the tinny sounds of 1920's jazz are coming from the coffee shop where a gaggle of excited, rain-soaked tourists, speaking rapidly in some foreign tongue—German, she thinks, or Swedish—have gathered around an assemblage of cast-iron tables and chairs.

She's wrong. The music, a spirited counterpoint to the rain's steady patter, is coming from the candle shop she's never noticed before now.

A sign just like the one over the courtyard's entrance hangs above the tiny shop's front door. From a few feet away, she can see the rows of identical candles lining each shelf in the front window. The glass containers are so large she could pick one up in both hands and her fingers would just barely touch around its circumference.

The smells get stronger as she approaches the shop's front door, and now that she's laid eyes on what is most likely their source, it's almost impossible to believe they contain essences of her husband and best friend. Whatever oils are mixed into these dark treasures, they've simply stirred memories deep within her. That's all—fresh, not-yet-buried-enough memories.

It would be intolerably rude of her to carry the dripping rolls of tapestry inside, and she fears leaning them against the front door would be just as inconsiderate. So she tries propping them against a column a few feet from the entrance, and is still jostling them into balance when a male voice behind her says, "You can bring them in if you want."

The man is handsome in a delicate, fine-boned way. He polishes the fog from his glasses with the edge of his vest while studying her casually at the same time; his lack of nervousness at her sudden presence suggests the confidence of a storeowner. Even in a neighborhood where people have a tendency to dress as if they've walked out of another era, there is a particular otherworldly elegance to his silk vest and tailored linen slacks.

"Oh, I wouldn't! They're soaked," she says.

"They're beautiful," he responds with a smile.

"Are they? I guess. Sure. I—I'm Cassidy Burke." She grimaces and jerks a shoulder in his direction to indicate she'd like nothing more than to shake his hand if her arms were free.

With another comforting smile, the man closes the distance between them and takes the wet rolls of tapestry from her arms before she can protest. She hates the thought of him dampening his immaculate outfit. But before she can stop him, he's upended all three rolls and placed them just inside the front door of his shop.

Inside, a thick Oriental carpet covers the hardwood floor, and the shelves along every wall are gleaming, varnished mahogany that matches the burnt-umber glass containers holding each candle. But the closer Cassidy looks at the candles, the more she can make out shades of purple amidst the brown. Is the wax one color and the glass containers another? Are the two shades working together to create an effect of syrupy, luxuriant darkness?

There's no counter or register, just a little desk pushed into one of the back corners where she spots a pile of receipts and a calculator. Several wheels of brightly colored ribbon are pinned to the wall above. The store's centerpiece is a round table with a black marble top and serpentine supports lined with flecks of ivory that curl upward like jeweled snakes united in the effort of holding the table's central column upright. There's a huge vase of yellow flowers, and beneath it a silver tray with a candle just like the one on the shelves. Only this one is lit, and the smells wafting from it have caused her face to flush. They're causing something else to happen as well, and she hopes, she *prays*, the store's owner hasn't noticed. But the rain has soaked her from her head to toe, turning her blouse into a wet napkin over her fiercely hard nipples.

"Cassidy?" *Shane asks. His tone is full of yearning, but she can't answer him back. Her head is spinning. Her heart is racing and there's a voice in her head that keeps crying,* It's happening! This is happening! *And she can't tell if this voice sounds joyful or if it's screaming words of warning. The way Shane strokes her breast feels hesitant and awkward at first. But then she realizes the little slips of his fingertips across the fabric of her blouse and bra have a purpose; he's searching for her nipple, searching for one of the seats of her deepest pleasure.*

They're best friends, have been since they were kids. She's never kept a secret from him, and he's never asked her a question she couldn't answer. But now…but now… Somehow just saying his name in response or saying "Yes, I'm here," *will feel as good as saying,* "Keep going. I want this. I've always wanted this so much."

Her husband's tongue traces a path up the opposite side of her neck, swirls beneath her earlobe. Then his hand slides up her thigh, squeezing—encouraging—and he takes her earlobe gently in his teeth. She shudders. Her sex ignites as if she's been penetrated and—

"Cassidy's Corner," the man says. "That's your shop, isn't it?"

Amazing how such a gentle voice could snap her back into the present so quickly. "It is," she says quietly. Her cheeks must be crimson.

"Lovely place. I've been in a few times. Of course, I'm not sure if you remember. Nor would I expect you to, what with the foot traffic around these parts. And it's possible the other lady was behind the register at the time."

There's no trace of New Orleans, or anywhere southern, for that matter, in his impeccable pronunciation. His manner of speaking is refined and utterly devoid of any regional accent, like a British actor who has trained himself for American television.

"Clara?"

"Yes. That was her name. Clara. Two C's—Cassidy and Clara. What a charming name that would make!"

"Maybe. But I can't afford to give Clara a cut of the profits, so I'll stick with Cassidy's Corner."

"Indeed," the man says, laughing gently. "I'm Bastian Drake. And now that your hands are free…" He extends his, and even though it feels rude, she studies it briefly before taking it. There doesn't appear to be a single line in the man's palm. Does he spend his evenings soaking his hands in some kind of essential oil? Or maybe he uses those silly gloves Shane tried to get her to sleep with every night until she woke up one too many times with one of them on her forehead and the other halfway down the covers, a slimy trail of moisturizer in its wake.

When she shakes Bastian's hand, she's afraid he'll be able to detect the arousal in her. Something about this fear makes her feel as if she's doing something morally questionable. She wonders if lingering in some tiny, otherworldly little shop with a beautiful man who appears to have stepped out of time constitutes some kind of infidelity. She feels a warm familiarity for Bastian Drake, but no desire—no *lust*. It's thoughts of her own husband the candle before her has stirred. That's all.

Oh, if only that were all, she chides herself. *If only it was* only *your husband you were thinking of right now.*

"Cassidy?" *Shane asks again. She's loves the halting sound of his voice, the gentle plea. He's always been a man of impulse and action. He is rough with other men, rough with everything—keys that jam, doors that get stuck. But with her, he has always taken his time and asked for permission. But never has he asked to do something like this.*

"Cassidy?"

Her best friend's breath against her neck, his hand on her breast, her husband gently kneading her thigh and nibbling her earlobe—when she tries to speak under the delicious assault of these pleasures, all that comes from her lips is a long, ragged sigh. And that's when Andrew grabs the back of Shane's neck. Before Cassidy can say her best friend's name, his lips have met hers, his tongue has slipped inside her mouth, and even though his throaty grunt sounds startled, he's rising up off the bench to meet the full force of her kiss, his hand leaving her breast and cupping the side of her face for the first time…

"Mr. Drake?"

"Yes, dear."

"What is *in* this candle?"

He smiles. "I believe the question is, what *isn't* in that candle?"

"A riddle. I see."

"Perhaps, but not quite," he says, laughing again. "It's probably not the best business practice to put it quite this bluntly, but I'm not your average candlemaker."

"I didn't know there was such a thing as an *average* candlemaker."

"Good point. What I mean to say is that in other stores you'll find various groupings of scents. Florals on one shelf, spices on another. Not here. Here, every candle is unique."

"Interesting marketing," Cassidy says.

"Perhaps, in that it involves faith."

"Faith?"

"Not in the religious sense, necessarily. But from my perspective, I must have faith that a particular scent will find the customer it needs to find."

"How often does it work?"

"It appears to be working right now," he says.

"May I?" she asks, fingering the edge of a label that folds over like a gift card.

Bastian Drake nods. She lifts one edge and reads the message written in calligraphic script inside:

Light this flame at the scene of your greatest passion and your heart's desire will be yours.

A shudder goes through her. She's not sure if it's fear or desire or both, but the innocent sounding invitation combines with the transportive effects of the scent. Suddenly she finds herself setting the candle back on the tray slowly and with a trembling hand.

"Take it."

Bastian Drake is next to her suddenly. His smooth, pale hand has closed over hers. The candle's glass base is frozen inches above the silver tray. She braces for a waft of his breath, but none comes. Indeed, the man gives off no smell at all. Where he held the dripping wet rolls of tapestry against his chest just minutes before, his Oxford and silk vest are smooth and dry.

"I can't..."

"Why not?" he asks.

"It's...." *Too much*, she wants to say. All of it is just too much. Its heady smells, the depth of feeling it stirs within her. It's the aromatic equivalent of a bittersweet song played on a lone violin, and each note animates a desire she would like to stay dormant, the desire to once again be at the center of the raw, animal passion of the two men who own her heart.

Bastian Drake's hand still rests atop her own. The candle's base still hovers inches above the silver tray. The flame is small, but it flickers steadily. It's hard to accept that such vivid memories of such raw desire can emanate from such a tiny, insignificant spark in the universe; a spark that doesn't waver in the drafts blowing through the shop's front door.

"My darling," he says quietly. "Take it from a man who passed up far too many gifts in his life. There is no virtue in ignoring your heart's desire. To deny it, perhaps, is a noble thing, if it will hurt others or betray a trust. But to ignore it is to condemn yourself to a lifetime of darkness."

They're standing so close now that if she turned to face him their proximity would seem inappropriate. Too intimate. But what could be more intimate than the words he just spoke into her ear? When he releases her hand, it feels as if a pressure wave has lifted from her arm. Before she can refuse his gift again, Bastian lifts the candle to his mouth, blows out the flame, and turns his back to her.

"This candle is yours!" he says brightly.

"How will I carry it? I—"

"I'll have someone bring it to your shop before the close of business."

"Mr. Drake, I'm not sure… How much is it? I know what rents are like around here and I don't expect you to—"

Bastian pulls a flattened gift box from a stack behind his desk. "Consider it a gift from one proprietor to another." But he won't look into her eye as he prepares the gift in question.

She'll risk offending him if she puts up any more of a fight, that's for sure.

The skill with which he fashions an elaborate, four-leafed bow out of turquoise and purple ribbon is as disarming as everything else in his shop. But the quickness of his movements suggest he just revealed more about himself than he expected to. Or maybe he thinks the sooner he gets her out of his store, the more likely she is to take the candle.

"The rain seems to have let up. I'd be a gentleman and help you carry those rolls back to your store but unfortunately I am a one-man operation."

"Of course. No. That's fine. Thank you. Mr. Drake, I'm sorry. But I'm just not sure if I should—"

When Bastian Drake finally looks her in the eye, Cassidy's first thought is that a passing car has bounced reflected light off the store's front window and it slid across Bastian's face. But they are facing the inside of a courtyard, not the street. Perhaps a bird flew by outside, or perhaps it's exactly what she doesn't want to believe it was. That some swell of emotion, some insistence within Bastian, caused a bright gold pulse to illuminate both of his eyes so briefly but so completely she's been rendered slack-jawed and frozen.

"Please," Bastian says quietly. "I insist."

Cassidy is surprised she can pick up the rolls of tapestry from where Bastian leaned them against the doorframe. She's surprised she can move her arms, or her legs, or her head. She expected to be hypnotized. She expected time to stand still or jump forward, because in films and T.V. shows that is what happens after someone bears witness to something as inexplicable and impossible as what she just saw. She isn't frightened, just hollowed out.

Is it possible to feel the thing they call suspension of disbelief toward your own life? Because as she hurries from the store, that's exactly what she feels. Between the candle's strange power and the inexplicable illumination within its maker, Cassidy Burke feels suddenly ready to believe anything.

2

"So it's a day for gifts, huh?" Andrew asks.

Cassidy is in the storeroom fashioning small blossoms out of the tissue paper she's just stuffed into a gift bag. Seconds earlier, Clara brought her the store's portable phone and tucked it between her ear and chin so she could continue working with both hands. Now her only employee is back behind the register, making cheerful small talk with their third customer of the day, a doctor from Birmingham who is about to plunk down three hundred dollars for an antique porcelain plate featuring an etching of St. Louis Cathedral.

"A day for gifts?" Cassidy asks. "I don't understand."

"Clara says some guy sent over a candle?"

"Oh. Yeah. That."

"Don't go breakin' my heart with some secret French Quarter love affair, Mrs. Burke," her husband says in a pronounced Georgia drawl.

He knows full well whenever he plays up the accent of his youth, Cassidy's lungs and thighs tend to open at the same time. Most of the Louisiana accents Cassidy grew up with sounded more East Coast than Deep South. Andrew is a native of Atlanta who fell in love with New Orleans, and her, during his undergraduate years at Tulane.

"You're the only man in my life, Andrew Burke. You know that."

She's issued this stock response time and time again over the years. This time it strikes a false note. The only sounds for the next few seconds are the steady rustle of her fingers molding tissue paper. *The only man in my life—except for that guy you made me kiss a few nights ago. Remember him? My best friend?*

Made her kiss him? That was hardly a fair description. It's not like she put up a fight or asked him to stop.

"So...the flowers?" Andrew asks.

"They're beautiful, as always."

"Yikes. I'm not boring you, am I?"

"No, I'm just busy right now, sweetie."

"I meant the flowers, Cassidy. My gestures of affection? I don't know. You sound less than thrilled."

The steady deliveries of lilies, lavender, and purple tulips have been far more than gestures of affection, she's sure of it. Every day since his Mardi Gras mischief, some new jaw-dropping bouquet has arrived just after lunchtime. And while they certainly make Cassidy's Corner smell better, they're also adding to her dread that the three of them—she, her husband, and Shane—did something dangerous, the consequences of which are somehow irreversible.

Her husband must be feeling a similar anxiety. He has ravished her the minute she's walked through the door every night since she's gone back to work, securing her in his powerful embrace, rattling off a series of politically correct questions ensuring her consent. Then, in the comfort of their bedroom, and their living room, and their front hallway, he's deployed all of her favorite perks: some ice cubes here, a silken wrist tie or two there, and always the intent and studied perfection with which he can devour her sex for what feels like hour after blissful hour. By the time he's done, she's too spent to bring up their little moment of weirdness at The Roquelaure House. (Even after spending most of their lovemaking wondering what it would be like to have Shane's lips and fingers join her husband's dutiful ministrations.)

"So any word from Superboy?" Andrew asks. He gave Shane this nickname when they were still in college, after Shane walked face-first into a sliding glass door at their beach house in Bay St. Louis. "The other night, you said you'd been texting him and he's been..."

"Ignoring me. Yeah. I remember."

She also remembers how quickly Andrew dismissed the topic when she did.

Probably sleeping off his hangover 'cause he spent the rest of Mardi Gras on Bourbon Street. Andrew's brusque response suggested he wasn't ready to talk about what they'd done together. So she dropped it. But she still doubted that's how Shane spent the remainder of the holiday.

Her best friend didn't party like he used to. Not since he'd moved out of that ridiculously overpriced condo in the Warehouse District so he could start investing some of the money his parents had left him. He'd also earned his real estate license and traded in his shiny little Boxster for a sensible Jeep Grand Cherokee more suited to driving clients around the city.

But Andrew's remark wasn't completely off base. For years, Shane was the twist of lemon in their Diet Coke; the guy who brought a bottle of Maker's Mark and some party hats to the hospital room after Andrew's hernia surgery. There had also been a few uncomfortable conversations about which one of Shane's friends was an appropriate guest at their more formal parties. (Gatherings of Andrew's fellow architects were not always the right setting for perpetually stoned tarot card readers who had never met a piercing they didn't like and porn star/dancer/models who had a tendency to go-go dance on any flat surface after consuming two beers.)

But those days were over. Shane Cortland was no longer a portal through which French Quarter eccentricity occasionally made flashy appearances in the midst of their buttoned-down, Uptown lives. These last few months the guy has seemed as career-focused and uptight as she and Andrew have been since graduating college. Cassidy couldn't remember the last time she'd accidentally awakened Shane with a mid-morning phone call on a weekday.

More importantly, Shane was not the one who got all three of them blasted on Kir Royales at a crowded Mardi Gras party at The Roquelaure House. Shane was not the one who steered them to an isolated bench before initiating a make-out session that had rendered her the white-hot center of their dual, drunken passion. That distinction belonged to her husband, Andrew Burke. And if the irony in that fact wasn't enough to make her head spin, Shane, the guy who'd spent most of his twenties seducing as many attractive gay men as he could (and a few straight ones), seemed to be more freaked out about it than either she or her husband.

Or so it seemed, if the smiley-faces, LOL's, and various other emoticons he'd been using to dismiss her text messages could be taken as evidence.

Was Shane, like her, lying awake most nights wondering what would have happened if they hadn't been interrupted by that drunken couple who had come stumbling down the garden path?

Does Shane remember feeling what she saw before it all came to an abrupt end—Andrew stroking the back of Shane's neck while he guided Shane's lips to his wife's mouth? *Her* mouth!

Jealousy should flood her at the memory of this physical intimacy between her husband and another man. Not a delicious heat on both sides of her neck; a heat that flows effortlessly across her cheeks, her lips, even her brow, without a single needle of fear dragging in its wake.

It's here, somewhere. She can't smell it. But she's sure it's to blame.

"*Clara!*"

The older woman's face appears around the curtain between the storeroom and the shop. "Yes?" she asks tightly.

"Where's that candle?"

"Up here, under the register. Would you like me to bring it back?"

"No, no. Just leave it up there. And…" Cassidy isn't quite sure what she wants to say next. *Be careful?* With a candle that doesn't weigh more than a pound?

"And what?"

"Nothing. I just wanted to make sure it was here."

"Sure," Clara finally says. "Okay."

"Cassidy…" Her husband's voice trails off. She knows that tone, pregnant with a sense of duty. And he just brought up Shane; she can feel what's coming. Her heart is racing faster than it did when Shane's hand kneaded her breast while Andrew's tongue traveled the nape of her neck.

"We should probably—"

"I need to go, sweetie. There's just a lot going on here right now."

And it's all going on in my head, but I can't talk about it. Because I'm not going to say I didn't want it, and I'm not going to pretend like I don't want more. But I'm terrified it will awaken something in you that I don't understand, something you've never acknowledged. Something I won't be able to control. As for me…?

"Sure, well, when you get home, maybe?" he asks. "You'll be home around six, right?"

"Around then. But wait—" Grateful to be off the hook if only for a few short hours, Cassidy reaches for her iPhone and opens her calendar. "Eight o'clock," she says, when she sees the appointment. "The Preservation Council's letting me set up a table at their luncheon but I have to get in there tonight so I'm not in the caterer's way tomorrow."

"Sounds good. Where are you setting up?"

The Roquelaure House. She bites back a quiet curse. *Well, if that isn't just the most—*

"I'm not sure yet. Clara has the info. Anyway, it should only take an hour or two."

"Sounds good," Andrew says suddenly. "I'll probably swim a few laps or something."

If she's not careful, the thought of her husband's muscular back slicing through their pool, powered by tan, sculpted arms, will have her as dizzy with desire as her visit to Bastian Drake's shop.

"Good. Glad someone's using the pool," she says. *Huh? What is she— his mother?*

"Yeah. Bye, babe. Tonight…"

"Yes. Tonight."

Unsure of what these final words even mean, she hangs up.

The tissue paper blossoms she's been forming with her hands look more like triffids than flowers. She feels like she just lied to her husband in a dozen different ways, none of them individually terrible. But in combination, they are enough to convince her she has to do something. They have to talk about what happened or they have to—

"Clara!"

"Yes."

"Can you bring me that candle?"

A few seconds later, Clara appears, the candle in both hands. She's grimacing. Cassidy has snapped at her twice now for no good reason— both times in front of a customer—and she's preparing to apologize when Clara sets the candle down with a loud *thunk*.

"Smells like pond water," Clara groans, then she picks up the customer's gift bag without being asked.

So it's the smell of the candle she hates.

Cassidy takes a whiff.

It's all here, just as it was that afternoon: vetiver, baking bread, musk—and *men*, there's just no other way to say it. *Her* men. And to Clara this all smells like pond water? One more suggestion that whatever happened inside of Bastian Drake's shop was as fundamentally strange as it felt.

Clara hovers. Cassidy feels the woman's stare as she lifts the label on the side of the glass container.

Light this flame at the scene of your greatest passion and your heart's desire will be yours.

"Remind me to take this with us when we go set up tonight," Cassidy says.

"Suit yourself, boss," Clara says.

Then the older woman is gone in a rustle of tissue paper and Cassidy is alone, staring down into the dark and inviting swirl of the candle's wax.

* * * *

"Are you sure?" Clara asks for the second time.

They're alone inside The Roquelaure House. The tables and chairs for tomorrow's luncheon were set up prior to their arrival. They fill the house's vast double parlor, but they're missing tablecloths and slipcovers, their exposed plastic and wood frames a stark contrast to the sparkling chandeliers and heavy, puddling drapes.

"I'll be fine," Cassidy answers. "You can go, seriously. I just need a few more minutes and then I'll lock up."

The display table for Cassidy's Corner is tucked into one corner of the room, next to a giant étagère filled with the Roquelaure family's pink and white china collection. The tablecloth she and Clara picked matches the china's color pattern almost exactly. She hopes this will make up for how small the table is.

Margot Burnham, the Preservation Council's iron-fisted chairwoman, insisted Cassidy employ the most unobtrusive presentation possible. Hence the small table, the limited collection of sale items, and a tent-sign so tiny and modest it looks like it should be reminding people not to smoke. Should Clara wander from her post tomorrow, it's likely the ladies of the council will stroll right past the spray of silver-plated mirrors, antique picture frames, and candles far smaller and less powerfully scented than the one from Bastian Drake, which is sitting on the floor next to one leg of the table, still inside the gold bag in which it arrived.

Over the years, Cassidy has attended countless fundraisers and parties inside this perfectly restored landmark home. The two-story Greek revival on St. Charles Avenue has also been used by dozens of television shows and movies, most of them stuffed with unbearable clichés about the city; constantly circulating trays of mint juleps, Cajun accents thicker than any you're likely to hear outside of the swamp, contemporary housekeepers dressed in the outfits of plantation slaves.

"Is everything all right, Cassidy?"

"It's fine. I just wish she'd let us bring a bigger table. But I guess it blends into the room in the end. Right? I mean, I can see Margot's point. She doesn't want it to look like we've crammed the entire store into her luncheon."

"Sure. It looks great. I'm just not that crazy about leaving you here by yourself."

"Oh, that's sweet, Clara. But really, I'm fine."

A streetcar passes, its low rumble echoing through the house's large, empty rooms, most of them vast warrens of shadow beyond the halos cast by the chandeliers overhead.

"Listen," Clara begins. "I just need to say there's a reason David and I spend Mardi Gras in Florida now. After a while, it gets so crazy."

"Clara, I'm not sure I understand…"

"I'm sorry, it's none of my business. But you've just been so in your head since we got back. And then all the flowers—I mean, I know you two went to all the parades and a bunch of parties. I thought maybe in all the wildness something might have, you know—*happened.*"

"Oh, no! That's sweet of you. But we're fine. I promise."

Wow. Not winning any Oscars for that *performance.*

It's awkward at times, being the boss to a woman twice her age, a woman who worked as a substitute teacher at Cassidy's high school. But never more awkward than it is right now, the two of them staring at each other expectantly, Clara gently chewing her bottom lip and absently rubbing the knuckles on her right hand back and forth across her neck.

"So he's meeting you here?" Clara whispers.

"Andrew's at home."

"No. Not Andrew…"

"Then *who?* Wait—you think I'm meeting *another* man here?"

"Oh, I don't know, Cassidy," she cries. "You've just been so strange!"

"Clara, I'm not cheating on my husband!"

"Well, it's such a beautiful house, Cassidy, and there are so many events here. I would hate for you to associate it with something you'd regret later."

She approaches Clara with her arms out. And in an instant, she's turned her half-hug into a single, steering arm clamped around Clara's upper back. She guides the woman toward the kitchen. "Clara, it is *so* sweet that you're this concerned for me—and for Andrew, and our marriage. But we're fine. Really. Everything's fine. And the event tomorrow will be fine, too, if you just go home and get some rest."

And maybe some wine and half a Xanax too, if it'll help you mind your own business.

"Are you sure?"

No. I'm not sure of anything right now except I have no plans to cheat on my husband. Unless we're counting, you know, candles.

"Yes. Of course."

At the back door, Clara gives her one last pleading look. "Text me when you get home. Just so I know you're safe."

"Of course, sweetheart. Of course."

She shuts the door as gently as she can, but it still feels as if she's slammed it hard enough to rattle every window in the house and seal herself inside for eternity.

3

ANDREW

We'll get through this, Andrew Burke thinks.

He soaps his hair frantically. The spray sends punishingly hot water sluicing down the hard ridges of his muscular back.

A little pain is good, he thinks. A little pain will help him forget the frosty phone call with his wife. And it's not like the water's scalding him. It's just hot enough to distract him from the terrifying prospect he might have destroyed his marriage.

If we got through that mess with Joe Lambert's secretary, we can get through this, I'm sure of it.

After all, what could be worse for your marriage than a beautiful woman in your office who won't take no for an answer? A woman who stops you in the parking lot and won't let you get by without forcing her to move—which, oh, by the way, means forcing you to *touch* her; a woman who makes things at work uncomfortable to the point of excruciating, leaving you no choice but to tell your wife about the situation because you don't want her finding out from someone else, and because you're a good husband and a good husband doesn't let a zone of secrecy grow around a beautiful young woman who can't take no for an answer.

All told, it was a six-month ordeal demanding constant uncomfortable conversations with Cassidy, his boss, and even a few lawyers when the woman threatened to make a false accusation against him. But at the end of the day, Andrew got through it without doing anything he might regret someday, all without having some chest-thumping meltdown over the fact that sexual harassment also happens to men and he was one of them.

He also didn't give in to temptation in the first place. It was easy to lose sight of that fact given how long the ordeal dragged on. It was also more than he could say for his old frat brothers, most of whom were in the process of breaking their own marriages.

Andrew, on the other hand, was a good guy. Better yet, he was a good husband. Why should those titles be revoked just because of a few minutes of crazy at some party?

Well, for starters, douchebag, *you actually* did *give in to temptation this time. So what if the temptation* involved *your wife? It was still—*

—*still* what? He tries to answer himself. *Forbidden? Hot? Inevitable?*

Thirty seconds.

That's how long he planned to spend in the shower. Just a quick rinse to get the product out of his hair, then a nice brisk swim to get the blood pumping. But he's been soaping his head now like a parent trying to delouse their child. Which is stupid because he barely styled his hair at all that morning.

When he'd first started working at Chaisson & Landry, he'd been an every-day-is-casual-Friday guy. Then Cassidy suggested to him that slacks, Oxfords, and a side part would probably earn him a little more respect from his colleagues, most of who are at least five years older than him. But every time she hands him a new tube of her favorite molding paste, she reminds him not to leave the stuff in when he goes to bed. Something about breakouts, she says. Letting the stuff smear across his face during a cross stroke probably isn't the best for his skin either, he figures, so he makes it a habit to wash his hair whenever he's about to hit the pool.

Truth be told, Andrew couldn't care less about his skin, which wasn't prone to acne even when he was a teenager.

No, what matters most to him is that his wife took the time to find the brand that smells the best, that she makes it a point to leave her book club early so she can pick up a replacement for him when he's running low. He doesn't want her to stop doing either of these things because he knows the smallest indicators of love can be the most important, the most lasting, and he figures the way to guarantee this is by following her grooming instructions to a tee so she can see how much her little ritual means to him.

Like now. For fifteen minutes. When she's not even home.

This is nothing, he thinks. *The whole thing. Just a little Mardi Gras...* He's still trying to complete this thought when he catches his own reflection in the steam-splotched mirror beyond the shower door. He's hard as a rock within seconds, a tendril of soapsuds dripping from the bobbing, glistening head of his cock.

Dude! Getting wood over your own reflection? Seriously?

But he stops laughing when he realizes what's really got him boned. Lately, it's become a trend, this *whole not seeing himself when he looks in the mirror* thing. Instead he sees the unconcealed lust that lights up Cassidy's eyes, and then Shane's, when they both catch an unexpected glimpse of his nearly nude body.

His instinct is to flick the suds away with one hand. But he knows if he so much as grazes his dick with his pinky he'll be instantly stroking himself to that hot but haunting memory from their trip to Bay St. Louis over Memorial Day weekend. A memory he's done his best to suppress for a year now, until a few too many Kir Royales at The Roquelaure House brought it bubbling to the surface.

A peaceful day at the Mississippi Coast, with the clapboard house bathed in the deep orange light of late afternoon and his family down at the beach (or so he thought). Just him, a nice long shower, and Ol' Blue Eyes crooning out of the surround speakers in the front room. Andrew was so sure he'd had the run of the place he decided to dance through every room as he toweled himself off, badly singing along with *That's Life*, before he barged in on Cassidy and Shane sipping coffee at the kitchen table while he polished his butt with the towel, his cock and balls swinging in the air in front of him.

The whole thing was a regular crack-up, for sure. They teased him about it for weeks, even nicknamed him *Mississippi Tarzan*, a nod to his terrible, off-key Sinatra impression.

But before the giggling and the friendly name-calling, there'd been a moment he didn't quite have a name for. A moment when his wife and her best friend had looked up from their coffee cups and surveyed his heat-flushed, naked body in the exact same instant. The combination of desire in their stares caused a stirring in his groin so powerful and immediate that by the time he spun from the room, the towel he was holding over himself like an embarrassed little boy hid an erection as throbbing and relentless as the one he was sporting now.

It wasn't the first time they'd done it to him either.

Freshman year at Tulane, the day he'd met them both. *Officially* met them both, after quietly stalking Cassidy for about a week. He just had to know more about the small blonde girl with the big, beautiful eyes, the one who listened quietly during their Intro to Philosophy discussion group before asking a single, precise question that would usually send the T.A. for a sputtering loop. One afternoon, he found Cassidy and some blond guy sitting together on the green, play wrestling and joking around with such casual intimacy he thought they might be boyfriend and girlfriend and he'd just come within inches of making an ass of himself.

But he wasn't sure, so he took a seat a few yards away and pretended to read *Slaughterhouse Five* while he studied them.

After a while, he thought they might be brother and sister. Twins, even, given their tendency to move in synch with one another. Suddenly, the guy sprawled out, hands raised skyward so Cassidy could grab on to them both while she tried to kick her legs up into the air behind her. Their giggling attempt at flight ended when her delicate body thumped down onto his lanky one. Entwined like rag dolls, Cassidy and Shane laughed so hard they briefly drowned out the repetitive strumming of the amateur guitarist a few yards away.

Then, as they righted themselves and brushed the grass off their clothes, Shane flicked both wrists before running his hands slowly through his soft, blond hair with the luxuriant tenderness of a woman showering in a shampoo commercial. *That dude's gay, even if she doesn't know it yet. Even if* he *doesn't know it,* Andrew thought. *I'm in!*

And then they both looked at him for the first time, the same look that would laser through him years later over Memorial Day weekend.

Their half-smiles fading as desire consumed their amusement, their eyes widening with lust as they examined him shamelessly from head to toe. And in that moment, they radiated a kind of *oneness* that suspended everything he knew to be true about labels or gender.

He had trouble putting a name to it, which was a shame, because he knew if he could name it, he'd be able to dismiss it, and if he could dismiss it, everything would be simpler. But there was no forgetting the way it made him feel; rock hard in his briefs, so hard he wanted to reach down and adjust himself—he couldn't; the back of his neck so hot suddenly he thought he might have moved into direct sunlight without realizing it—he hadn't. And then there was that delicious, anticipatory pressure in his temples, like a head massage from a guardian angel, the same anticipatory pressure he feels whenever Cassidy whispers something naughty in his ear during a stolen moment at dinner with his colleagues.

Sometimes he compares it to that scene in *Ghostbusters* when they all crossed the streams of their ray guns to defeat the evil spirit living atop that old New York apartment building. Only he was no monster, and the raw hunger their combined gaze filled him with was nothing like defeat. It made him feel powerless, for sure, and helpless before a desire he couldn't name. But not defeated.

Defeated is how he feels now, as he drip-dries in the cooling air outside the shower stall, willing his cock to go down.

He's not gay. There's no doubt about that. Sure, there'd been those late nights of sleepover experimentation with Danny Sullivan back in high school. But that was different. They'd been best friends since they were kids. And yes, parts of it had been fun, even hot. Mostly the parts where Danny's racing heart and shivering body made it clear he'd always wanted to explore Andrew's body more than he'd let on. In those moments, making Danny happy had made *him* happy, happy enough to get him hard. And keep him hard. And really, how hard was it to get a man hard anyway?

He'd shared all of this with Cassidy during the full-disclosure period of their engagement. When she wasn't shocked, he was shocked. He was even more shocked when she told him every guy she'd been serious with had eventually admitted to fooling around with another guy at some point in his life. But none of that mattered now. What mattered was that nothing about his late nights with Danny Sullivan had left Andrew with a burning desire for other men. In fact, he couldn't remember a single moment when he'd laid eyes on a strange man and thought, *Damn, I'd hit that*. But just to be sure, he's checked out some gay porn sites, studied a few hardcore photos to see if any of them trigger a part of him that's blossomed over the past few years. Everything he sees there leaves him cold. For starters, there are no women at all, and that's a big problem, and secondly, none of the guys are Shane. None of the rutting, passionless couples he studied have the combined charge of his wife and her best friend.

It's simple, really. Or at least it should be.

Shane is the other half of the woman he loves more than anything in the world. When he was younger, this fact used to make him insanely jealous. Now it fills him with hunger. Because now he's almost as close with Shane as he is with his own wife, except for the part where they...

How could he *not* feel something for the—

Andrew slams both palms down on the side of the counter, hard enough to knock a bottle of contact lens solution onto its side.

Get in the goddamn pool before you rub one out in the bathroom like some horny teenager.

4

CASSIDY

The bench looks the same, perhaps a bit lonelier given there isn't a party in full swing nearby.

Cassidy is surprised her fevered memories didn't exaggerate its slender design or its cast-iron frame. It's in the same spot, beneath the spreading branches of a massive oak, hemmed in by a small perimeter of banana trees sprinkled with uplights. String lights from the party still wrap the oak tree's branches overhead, but they're turned off and probably have been since the event.

The few floors she can see of the condo high-rise next door are dark. A streetcar lumbers by on St. Charles Avenue, its clatter muffled by curtains of foliage. There are scrapes and rustles from the plants nearby, but the loudest sound she hears is the sound of her own breathing as she tugs a matchbook from her pocket.

The candle rests on the flagstones at her feet. She's taken care to stuff the tissue paper back inside the bag and set it aside. She's about to light the match when another thought hits her and suddenly she's pulling her phone from her pocket and setting it on the bench beside her. Now that she's done it, she's not exactly sure why. Maybe she fears the candle will poison her; a few less inches between her and 911 might mean the difference between life and death. It did nothing of the kind while it burned inside Bastian Drake's shop. But this is different. Now she's poised to obey the instructions written on the candle's tiny card; she's going to light the thing at the scene of her greatest desire. Who knows what will follow? The whole thing could be a terrible trick.

Maybe, but how much help could dialing 911 be if it is?

Enough stalling.

The match doesn't light after three strikes.

A little act of self-sabotage, she thinks, bringing a matchbook instead of a cigarette lighter. Then the match lights suddenly. Before she realizes what she's done, she's brought the flame to the candle's wick and shaken the match out with one hand.

She sits back, preparing herself for—she's not sure what exactly. Perhaps a stronger tide of the candle's intoxicating scents?

But what comes next is something else entirely.

At first, she assumes a cloud of delicate, luminescent insects have flown into the halo of the candle's growing flame, circling like lazy moths. But the candle's surface also glitters and glows. The wax looks like a piece of thin mesh stretched over a puddle of hot lava. And the swirl of particles above are fed by little sparkling flecks that drift up into the air, determined embers driven by an impossible, upward wind.

The smell hits her next, far more powerfully than what she experienced in Bastian Drake's shop. She is instantly, fiercely moist. A great wave of pressure has forced her back against the bench. But with this pressure comes pleasure as well, coursing through her with such intensity— it feels as if several sets of hands are caressing her, massaging her body from head to toe. Her nipples are aflame. She can hear herself laughing, the kind of high-pitched, nervous laughter that usually rips from her when Andrew surprises her in the shower with a forceful tongue and a throbbing erection.

As she catches her breath, she sees the golden column above the candle's flame. It towers over her now, at least seven or eight feet tall. Its celestial light bathes the undersides of the thick oak branches above. The glittering particles swirling madly through the body of the column take on distinct shapes.

Bare shoulders, the napes of necks, faces turned away from her—three apparitions appear inside the candle's impossible golden halo, each one worshiping the tiny flame below. As they gain definition, they rise higher toward the branches above, sloughing off more sparkling tendrils.

Their naked backs are turned to her as they spin. Cassidy sees a woman and two men, their heads bowed, their foreheads practically touching, as if they're all staring down at the candle that gave them impossible life. It looks as if they've been placed on a hovering, spinning dais composed of the candle's smoke and light. They rise higher into the air, growing in size beyond any proportion that could be called human.

Then, some threshold is crossed. Suddenly all three figures lift their heads and gaze into each other's eyes. But there is only a deeper shade of gold beneath their eyelids. And while their expressions are serene, the display should be terrifying, this sudden life force that courses through figures that were mere silhouettes just seconds before. But the woman in the trio doesn't look like Cassidy at all, and for some reason Cassidy is too startled by this fact to be afraid. The two men don't look like Andrew and Shane either. She doesn't recognize their faces at all.

Both men peel away from the column before Cassidy can study them further. They lose their human shape, columns of glittering gold, rocketing skyward, the branches slicing through them as they ascend.

Cassidy is alone with the remaining sprit. Almost as tall as the oak branches overhead now, the woman has tuned her placid smile and glittering gold eyes on the bench—and on Cassidy. If it wasn't for that peaceful, welcoming expression, if it wasn't for the warm and welcoming color of her impossible form, Cassidy would be terrified of this…*ghost? Spirit? Angel? What is it?* Who *is it?*

Cassidy has no time to decide. Suddenly, the ghostly woman's face collapses. Her body becomes a single sheet of glittering gold that crashes silently over Cassidy's body like snow in a downdraft. A shuddering orgasm that's been building in her since she first lit the candle explodes inside of Cassidy. She hears her ecstatic cries as if from a distance.

When the darkness returns, it feels as if a blanket has been drawn around her. In contrast to the blinding wash of gold, the garden's ordinary shadows suddenly feel like a jarring supernatural event.

Cassidy shudders and gasps. It feels as if the woman's spirit moved right through Cassidy from her toes to her head, gently dragging her fingertips along every pleasure center in Cassidy's body during the trip.

A stab of guilt tries to pierce the layers of bliss, but fails. An orgasm without her husband? It's not like she was truly alone. Not really. Two other spirits just rocketed skyward, very much like the one that has left her thighs in spasms. But she knows right where they're headed; she's sure. Or *who* they're headed for. The idea that Shane and Andrew may soon share in this intense, ethereal delight fills her with joy. Not just joy, but also a wild and unrestrained hunger for them both.

5

ANDREW

With each stroke, Andrew hopes Cassidy will return home before he exhausts himself. When she does, he'll pull her into the pool by one arm, peel her wet blouse from her breasts with his teeth, grip her hips and squeeze just a little so that her back will arch and her sex will rise up toward him through the bathtub warm water.

In the meantime, he risks temptation swimming in the nude like this. Each time his bare ass breaks the surface, each time water rushes across his cock and balls when he turns off one wall, he's tempted to seize his erection in one iron-fisted grip and finish himself off. But he's saved himself for his wife every night since the incident. It feels like the right thing to do. But it wasn't easy. Especially during long days at the office, when the memory of her gasps as Shane devoured her neck would have him eyeing the only private bathroom at the office to see if he could steal a few minutes of self-release.

Not then, not now. *Save it up, mister. Stroke. Breathe. Stroke. Breathe. Find another word for stroke. Breathe. Find another word for stroke, seriously. Now.*

Their swimming pool is a long, slender rectangle that takes up most of their backyard. To keep the neighbors from getting an eyeful, he left the pool light off. Same story with the row of gas lanterns along the brick wall that hides the neighbor's house.

He installed the lanterns himself, which required him to learn more about gas-powered fixtures than he thought it was possible to know. So when the lantern closest to him pops to life like a miniature Olympic torch, the wrongness of the sound halts Andrew in mid-stroke.

They don't come on one at a time. That's not how they work. You hit the switch, and then you wait a few seconds while clicking sounds indicate that gas is being fed down the length of the line. Then all four lanterns flicker to life, gently, sometimes so weakly it looks like they're not going to catch. Never one by one, never with a loud, obtrusive *pop*.

But it happens again. And again. And again, until all four lanterns are lit. An impenetrable radiance fills the glass chambers of each lantern. He can't see the tiny gas flames anymore, just a bright halo of yellow. Fingers of bright gold have emerged from each lantern. They rise snakelike through the night air before converging at the end of the swimming pool, just above the steps to the shallow end. Their movement is steady, determined, unswayed by the humid breezes rippling the pool's surface. Treading water, his rasping breaths the loudest sound in the entire yard, Andrew watches as the glistening, gold tendrils of material he doesn't have a name for form the vague outline of a...*ghost?*

But ghosts are not made of gold.

They're also not real, jackass.

Then the smell hits him and Andrew Burke thinks, *I'm dying. That's it.* And then he thinks, *Dying smells incredible, like every delicious scent I've ever discovered on my wife's body, the floral notes of her perfume mingling with the scent of her juices, a combination of lilac—and candle wax.*

The figure standing at the edge of the swimming pool is not human. Human beings aren't hollow. When they open their eyes, you see pupils and irises, not golden sclera. It's a *he*, for sure, with handsome, defined facial features, but the rest of his identity is a mystery, and wondering about his identity seems insane given that he doesn't have a real body, just a glittering, shifting suggestion of one.

The figure goes down on one knee, lowers one glittering finger toward the surface of the water. But his face is angled upward. Andrew realizes this spirit, this golden ghost, is staring at him expectantly.

"What are you?" Andrew whispers.

He's answered by another burst of intoxicating scents. Only now there's a new smell—it's vaguely sandalwood, earthy. It's Shane. It's both of them, essences of Cassidy and Shane entwined in this impossible bouquet. It washes over him with invisible, overpowering force. The shimmering figure is still down on one knee. One glittering finger, shedding tiny particles of bright gold like delicate embers, still hovers just above the pool's surface.

Waiting, Andrew thinks. *Whoever, whatever, he is, he's waiting for my permission.*

"Yes," Andrew whispers.

Instantly, the golden ghost touches one finger to the water. Andrew watches in astonishment as two glittering snakes of light travel under the surface of the pool.

The nearer they come, the more his cock hardens. Then suddenly he feels himself lifted as if a whale is passing directly under him. Pleasure courses through his body from head to toe. The smells of Cassidy and Shane fill his nostrils; they bathe the back of his throat.

Andrew realizes the sparkling gold tide hasn't moved around him and that can only mean one thing.

No, not possible, he thinks. *I'd be in pain, terrible pain. At least, at first. Cassidy's never even put a finger down there.* And it was so fast, and there was no resistance. But the shimmering gold waves are gone now, and there's nothing outside of him that could be sending these waves of radiant pleasure through his limbs. It feels like he's being massaged by several sets of hands. Two sets of hands. But the pressure inside of him is something else altogether; it moves to a different, more powerful rhythm. It was outside of him before, but now it's inside. His balls have drawn up so tightly he knows exactly what's coming next, but he can't believe it. Only one person's ever been able to do this to him with the touch of her hand. Well, two people, if you count *him.* But never, not once, has he ever been able to do what's about to happen without touching—

His seed jets from him. He's so dumbfounded he looks down into the water, tries to watch it happen with his own two eyes. But it's too dark and the orgasm is so powerful it knocks his knees out from under him. When he throws his head back, his scalp touches the water's surface. Will the pleasure literally drown him if he doesn't get control? He flails madly to right himself. But even as he tries to stand firm in waist-deep water, he bellows.

And then, when his breath returns, he gasps the word that was on his lips that night at The Roquelaure House, that word he didn't have the courage to voice then as he watched his wife and her best friend kiss passionately for the first time, a word that filled him with excitement and arousal and satisfaction as he beheld the oneness, the beauty of Cassidy and Shane together at last.

"Mine," Andrew whispers.

6

SHANE

"Are you out of your goddamn mind, Shane Cortland?"

"Easy!" Shane hisses.

"Easy, *nothing.*"

Samantha Scott glances around the restaurant to see if her outburst attracted attention from any of the other diners. It did, but she doesn't seem to care. Before Shane can catch his breath, she's back to glaring at him as if he just informed her, a few bites too late, that her shrimp remoulade has magic mushrooms in it.

The wall behind her is covered in antebellum portrait paintings, Civil War muskets, and a succession of gilt-frame mirrors reflecting the crowded dining room. It's certainly an ironic image; the sight of his black transgender friend, decked out in a banded plunge-V Donna Karan dress the color of Merlot, sitting before a collage of artifacts from the slave days. On any other night, Shane would get a kick out of it. But right now, he's so surprised by Samantha's anger he can barely look her in the eye.

Perry's occupies both floors of an old French Quarter carriage house and its expansive courtyard. The most popular tables are outside next to the fountain. But they're sitting inside because he wanted to talk over things with Samantha in peace. He didn't expect the place to be quite so packed. It's a weeknight, after all. He also didn't expect Samantha to pitch an epic fit when he told her about a wayward moment of sexual fluidity with Cassidy and Andrew.

His veal cutlets swim in some of the finest beurre blanc he's ever tasted. But the slow burn of Samantha's anger incinerates his appetite. She's crossed her hands over her lap like a prim schoolteacher. She's shaking her head and taking deep, dramatic breaths through both nostrils. The only thing she's missing is a Bible and a fan.

"Lord, girl," he mutters. "Calm down."

"She is your *best* friend," Samantha whispers.

"Yeah, well, maybe *you'll* replace her."

"He's her husband."

"Yeah, and *he* started it. Not me. So lighten up already."

"Dark and proud, thank you. It's the one thing God got right the first time."

"Samantha, of all people, I didn't think you would be so judgmental."

"Oh, what? You think 'cause I'm your trans friend that I'm just gonna sit back quietly while you juggle knives? Listen here, Shane. Secrecy is not how the heart operates. Take it from someone who used to wait just a *little* too long to tell a boyfriend my birth certificate said *Stanley* Scott!"

"Wait. What *secrecy*?"

"You telling me you never made a move on Cassidy's husband?"

"*Never.* Oh my God! Andrew? Are you kidding? He's her husband."

"He's also *fine!*"

"Yes, and I love Cassidy and I have a conscience, thank you very much."

"So it just came out of the blue? Andrew has too much to drink and suddenly all three of y'all are making out together at some party?"

"Basically."

"*Basically?*"

How can Shane answer this? *Out of the blue…* They're his best friends, for Christ's sake. He can't think of any two people in the world he's closer to, can't think of anyone who knows more of his secrets than Cassidy *and* Andrew. But there was one secret they didn't know. Samantha didn't know it either. Because no one knew. No one except for the couple he'd shared that furtive afternoon with, on the carpeted floor of the penthouse he'd just sold them. Because they hadn't just been a couple. They'd been his clients, for God's sake. And the three of them had done a helluva lot more than make out for a few minutes on some garden bench.

His cheeks are so hot he contemplates pressing some ice cubes from his water glass to his face. Now he's struggling to sift through a decade's worth of memories looking for signs that this—he still doesn't have a name for it; they're all too scary—was always in the making, the eruption of a long-denied passion that's simmered just below the surface for years.

But Shane is sure of one thing -- Andrew Burke isn't gay.

He's known his fair share of closet cases. Cassidy's husband isn't one of them. No man can fake the adoration and desire Shane sees in Andrew's dark eyes every time he looks at his wife. There's nothing hesitant or forced about the way Andrew grabs Cassidy right in front of him, tickles her on the hips until she collapses in hysterics onto the sofa and smothers her with kisses until she blushes fiercely and asks him to stop because Shane is still in the room.

Did Andrew shoot him a look in those moments Shane didn't read properly? An invitation Shane read as a dismissal?

Hell, maybe that was Andrew's real motive the other night. He wanted Cassidy right then in the middle of the party, and he couldn't be bothered to get rid of Shane first.

But that's absurd! Andrew had been focused on something else entirely during those feverish moments; Cassidy and Shane together, in front of him, under *his* direction. Andrew had wanted those things badly enough to risk the closeness and connection the three of them had built together over the years.

And where had Shane's focus been? On Cassidy, on the feel of her opening, on her racing heart as she offered him the one thing she's never given him, and on Andrew's firm, forbidden grip on the back of his neck.

And maybe that's where he should be looking for signs. Not with Andrew, with Cassidy. Forget Mardi Gras and The Roquelaure House. Try that afternoon last year, when he and Cassidy had been snuggling together on her bed, marathoning reruns of *The Golden Girls*, and suddenly the supple curve of her bare foot had seemed so inviting he dragged one finger across it.

When she squealed and drove her body back against his, something about her vulnerability and frenzied pleasure had started an engine inside of him, an engine that drove him to take her in his arms and flip her onto her back. But once he got her there, once he had her squealing and panting and trying to bat his hands away, a voice in his head had said, *Stop*. The same voice he'd heard that day freshman year of high school, when the sight of Brent Parker running sprints on the football field, his tan skin glistening with sweat, had made Shane feel hungry and tingly and sad all at the same time, a voice that had said, *It's wrong. You don't like any of the names for that feeling. So quit it!*

Years later, he didn't release Cassidy as quickly as he'd looked away from Brent Parker that day. But Shane had been just as startled, just as frightened. It felt like he'd stumbled across a deeper current of desire. But that wasn't right either; it had swept him up without warning. There were unexpected consequences to touching Cassidy in certain ways. How could that be? There was more there, it seemed. And he thought he'd reached a point in his life where if it seemed like there was *more* there with someone, you leaned into it, you didn't pull away. But this was Cassidy. This was different.

"Order a drink," Samantha says and slams her own down onto the table to get his attention back.

"I don't drink during the week."

"Start. It'll clear your head."

"Is this your way of apologizing?"

"For what?"

"For accusing me of trying to break up my best friend's marriage."

Samantha rolls her eyes, lifts a bite of shrimp to her mouth and chews delicately while she considers her response.

Shane's appetite has yet to return.

"You remember Jonathan Claiborne? Used to be a waiter here?"

"Of course I do."

"You hooked up with him, didn't you?"

"I did."

In the past, Shane would have enjoyed remembering his no-strings-attached assignation with one of the hottest guys in New Orleans. Jonathan's smooth, rock-hard body bearing down on his, the man's skillful tongue swirling down the length of Shane's cock, suckling his balls before tickling the edge of his taint while he looked up to gauge the depth of Shane's blissful response with a broad, bright-eyed smile. But now these lustful remembrances do nothing to lighten Shane's current mood.

Or maybe it's something else, he wonders.

When compared to the raw passion he unleashed with Cassidy and Andrew, his hookup with a notorious local hottie seems sort of sweet, but not all that appetizing. Like taking a bite of hard candy and realizing you're chewing more plastic wrap than sugar.

"He's missing," Samantha announces.

"Jonathan?"

"Yep. No one's heard from him for weeks."

"I thought he quit."

"He did and rumor has it he got another job. As a call boy."

"Are you joking?"

"Nope. Quits his job here, starts selling what he's got, suddenly no one knows where he is."

"And you think something bad happened to him?"

"I think he needed to be *special*. I think it wasn't enough for him to just be gorgeous and get up every morning and go to work. He had to wring every last dollar out of what God gave him because being Jonathan Claiborne wasn't enough. He had to go turn himself into the spice in someone's cocktail. And now who knows what happened to him 'cause of it?"

"You're losing me here, Sam."

"Fine. Let me put it this way. I didn't transition so that I could be some magical drag queen people hire for parties. I wanted a foundation of truth under me, Shane. And you deserve the same. What is it those two call you again? The twist of lemon in their Diet Coke?"

Those two, he wants to say. *These are my* best friends *we're talking about.* But instead he says, "Don't be their little experiment. Is that what you're saying?" he asks.

"Exactly. 'Cause when they're done with you, they'll have each other. And you'll have no one."

As usual, Samantha's given eloquent voice to an internal monologue that's tortured him for days. But her logic crashes up against the fevered memories of those few minutes of shocking intimacy like waves hitting a seawall.

Of course everything Samantha has said makes sense.

But for Christ's sake, he's not some random gay dude Cassidy and Andrew met in a bar on vacation and tried fooling around with just to, you know, *see.*

He's their... He is their... Has there ever been a name for what the three of them share?

Third wheel is an insult, and it does nothing to describe their evident love for him. *Friend* is too safe and it barely suggests the amount of time they spend together. And *best friend to a couple* doesn't exactly trip off the tongue.

What's the word for two friends who show up on your doorstep at a moment's notice when the guy you've been dating for a few weeks freaks out on you because he's been sneaking shots of GHB behind your back and you were too dumb to notice? What's the word for the couple who doesn't ask a single question when you call them in a terror, your voice shaking, because you just made the guy leave and on his way out he turned over a lamp, kicked the door frame a few times, and then after you slammed the door behind him, he punched it not once, but twice, and shouted, *I'll be back, you little bitch*?

What do you call the sense of total safety Shane felt as Cassidy sat with him on the sofa, her hand in his, while Andrew checked all the windows and locks in his apartment? How can he describe the feeling in his heart—a lightness, an openness, a kind of lift—when neither one of them rushed out the door that night, when they offered to stay with him until he managed to relax? And when he woke up the next morning entwined in their arms, his nose resting in the nape of Andrew's neck while Cassidy's head rested on his chest, the early morning news playing on a television they'd all fallen asleep watching—what should he have called the combination of hunger and satisfaction the dual press of their bodies awakened in him?

If you're looking for a sign of what was to come, he thinks, *looks like you just found it.*

"Bathroom break," Shane mutters.

"Shane!" Samantha calls after him, regret stitching her features.

He waves at her to indicate he's okay, but just this small gesture makes his head spin.

Shane locks himself in the bathroom, grips both sides of the porcelain sink, and tries to get some breath into his lungs.

He's desperate to blame someone for his current confusion, someone besides Andrew or Cassidy. Or himself. And the only people he can think of are that damned couple, Mike and Sarah Miller.

7

They hadn't just been clients of his. They'd been his very first clients, and he'd figured their flirtations had just been meant to put him at ease. That's how nervous he'd been during their first day together, apologizing incessantly whenever his cell phone rang, stumbling over his feet in his rush to open every door.

Relax, kid, their lingering smiles and gentle squeezes seemed to say. *Pretend like we're just the cool parents of one of your friends, and not hard-to-please multi-millionaires looking for their perfect New Orleans getaway.*

Besides, they'd both seemed super conservative, hardly the type to initiate what came later. Mike Miller was a high-ranking former military man who'd made a bundle off defense contracts; the guy was a man's man by any generation's definition, gym built, with a high-and-tight haircut and a handshake so firm it could break a wine glass. So what if he liked to give Shane a little wink whenever his wife wasn't looking? Some straight guys have goofy ways of ending a sentence—it was better than a thumbs-up, right?

While her husband charged his way into each room with intense focus, Sarah Miller seemed to float in behind him on a cloud of Chanel. She sported a lustrous mane of golden hair and a perfectly even, store-bought tan. Each time they met, she wore low-cut, sleeveless dresses so shiny and well tailored they probably cost as much as Shane's Jeep. And then there was that husky voice that gave Shane a fluttery feeling in his chest every time she called him *honey.*

Nerves, he'd told himself. *Don't read too much into anything. It's just nerves.*

Besides, maybe clients were always touchy-feely when they wanted you to find them the perfect condo. He tried to get another agent at the firm to buy into this explanation, but the woman laughed in his face instead. "Are you high?" she barked. "Most clients treat you like you're a waiter who screwed up their order five times."

So he shouldn't have been all *that* surprised by what happened when he met the Millers to hand over the keys to their new penthouse.

As soon as the gorgeous couple took a few steps across the threshold, a long silence fell. Shane took that as his cue to leave. But when he opened his mouth, he saw Sarah Miller's gaze roaming the length of his body with undisguised lust.

"What do you say we really close the deal, honey?"

The line sounded lifted from a porn film. And he didn't think women as classy and elegant as Sarah Miller watched porn films. But he wasn't going to say that out loud, not in a million years. Which was a good thing because he couldn't bring himself to say anything at all.

The last time Shane could remember being so aroused he was a teenager and he'd finally worked up the nerve to download a video of two men going at it. Only rarely since then had he felt this same cascade of devastating sensations. The sides of his face felt tingly and numb. A radiant heat spread through his chest. His heart raced so fast he could feel his pulse beating in his ears. And all they were doing was looking at him. Looking at him like they wanted to devour him. Like they wanted to own him— *together.*

"Oh…" It sounded more like a hiccup than an answer, and the couple before him smiled in unison. Then Michael Miller clamped one hand around the back of Shane's neck and pushed him knees-first to the plush carpet. In stunned disbelief, Shane looked up. Mike gave him a warm, half-smile, and freed his thickening cock from his trousers. And then it was filling Shane's mouth and throat. Dizzy from the depravity of it all, he couldn't remember the last time a man had tasted so good, so forbidden.

He had a few gay friends who'd tried threeways with men and women. They'd all told the same story; the minute the woman laid a tender hand on them, bye-bye boner. But that's not what happened when Sarah Miller ran her fingernails up the back of Shane's neck as he suckled her husband's cock. Lightning bolts of pleasure shot up his spine. And after she sank down behind him and carefully unbuttoned his pants, the light scrape of her fingernails as she stroked his shaft felt deliciously exotic.

Then she was on her feet, staring down at him as he slathered her husband's erection with attention. She looked radiant with desire and power. Was it just lustful gratitude he felt? She had, after all, just given him her husband's throbbing, perfectly sculpted cock. When he ran his hands gently up her thighs, pushing the hem of her dress upward in the process, he told himself it was just to thank her. But when he saw her glistening, exposed pussy, saw that she hadn't worn panties in preparation for this very event, his gesture of gratitude turned to unexpected, overpowering hunger.

His first slow, exploratory sweep of his tongue managed to find her clit right at the end. She let out a cry that was as much surprise as bliss—maybe she didn't expect him to go both ways—then she was grasping the back of his head, guiding him back and forth between her husband's cock and her throbbing folds.

Eventually they tumbled to the carpet, breathless, and in the minutes that followed Shane was their ravenous, oral plaything, the taste of Mike Miller's musk blending with the earthy tang of Sarah Miller's flowing arousal on Shane's unstoppable tongue.

In the few moments when Shane didn't leave them gasping for breath, Mike managed to yank his wife's dress down far enough to free her breasts, sucking feverishly at her nipples while Shane deep-throated his cock. By adding Shane to the mix, the married couple had made their bodies taste and feel new to each other again. When Shane added two fingers to the dance of his tongue across Sarah's swollen nub, her orgasm shattered her, leaving her growling and clawing at the carpet on either side of her spread legs. Then Mike was on his feet, pulling Shane's head back as he furiously stroked himself to the edge. Shane fought the desire to open his lips, to take the man's load into his mouth. But the man was a stranger, and some rules still applied.

And then it was over.

No chitchat. No small talk. Just over.

The married couple dressed as if they'd just been woken up from a nap, both of them practically tripping over themselves to avoid Shane's eyes whenever he glanced nervously in their direction.

There weren't a lot of cleanup options; there was no furniture in the place yet, let alone hand towels. But still, the perfunctory manner in which Mike Miller pulled a roll of paper towels from a cabinet and handed it to Shane so he could wipe the man's cum off his face didn't feel deliberately degrading with the intent to arouse. It felt simply dismissive.

You're excused, kid. Sarah and I will now return to normal, heterosexual married programming.

Shane was no stranger to quick, no-strings-attached hookups with other men; he'd fled from all manner of French Quarter apartments at all hours of the night. But to have a kettle of new feelings and desire set to boil by such a sudden, ferocious explosion of lust, and then be cast out immediately afterward—it was more than he could take. And when he finally made it back to his Jeep, after he fastened the seat belt and stuck the keys into the ignition with a trembling hand, he was astonished to find himself blinking back tears. He couldn't remember the last time he'd cried after sex, but that's exactly what he was doing as the few spots of Mike Miller's cum he'd missed started to dry on his face. The Millers had left him as confused and frightened and vulnerable as a deflowered virgin, and here he was, crying alone in his car like some idiot.

But it wasn't just sex he was crying over. It was something more. An awakening he'd never expected, and at the end of the day, it didn't have much to do with Mike or Sarah Miller.

It wouldn't be like that with Cassidy and Andrew. It would be—

But he didn't finish the sentence. *Wouldn't* finish the sentence. *Could never in a million goddamn years finish that sentence.* It was impossible. It was insane. If his head and his heart felt this scrambled after a meaningless threeway with some clients, he didn't want to imagine how crazy he'd be after—

Cassidy pulled her dress back for him, displaying the most secret parts of herself for him, after Andrew took the back of Shane's head in his grip, giving him permission to taste the cock he's been given only brief glimpses of over the years. After he tasted both of them, together. And then after, the two of them holding him, not handing him a roll of paper towels. Holding him in their arms like they did that night he called for their help against that druggie he'd just thrown out of his apartment.

He slammed the sides of both fists against the steering wheel, hard enough to make the horn bleat.

At least he'd stopped crying.

And that's what he does now, weeks later, in the bathroom at Perry's, slams his fists against both sides of the sink. Only there's no car horn he blows by mistake this time. Just the porcelain basin, and it's a lot harder than his Jeep's steering wheel. But a little physical pain is exactly what he needs to stop him from rifling through his entire sexual history looking for more evidence that he hasn't always been the man he thought he was.

Then he looks up and sees a golden ghost staring back at him from the mirror.

8

Shane makes a sound like he's been kicked in the stomach.

When the edge of the toilet slams into the back of his legs, he realizes he jumped backward several feet. Too many things are happening at once for him to make sense of a single one. Threads of gold dust sail out from the four-foot tall mirror as if the glass weren't there at all, as if the gilt frame bordered a window. Before the ghost vanishes entirely, Shane glimpses its vague, shifting features.

Jonathan Claiborne...

A hallucination, for sure. It has to be! Samantha just mentioned the guy so it sort of makes sense. There was something in his food, Shane thinks. Or maybe the stress of the past few days has triggered some kind of psychotic break.

That's all well and good, he thinks, but how does he explain the two long fingers of gold now circling the artichoke-shaped light fixture overhead? Suddenly the fixture comes free, as if a giant hand just tugged it gently from the ceiling.

Shane's hands fly out to catch it before it shatters to the floor. But the intricate glass light fixture doesn't fall. It floats, descending slowly before it lands softly in his outstretched palms. The scents hit him next, so powerful they distract him from the fact that he's rising off the floor. Baking bread, lilac: the combination is familiar. He is engorged within seconds, gasping with as much pleasure as fear.

He spins in place, several feet in the air, the large light fixture balanced in his open palms by the same otherworldly force that pulled it free of the ceiling. It hasn't broken, this precious, intricate piece of glasswork. The prospect of it shattering at his feet was a greater fear than any he'd ever experienced. But it's being supported now—and *he's* being supported, too, by golden fingers of thick and fluid light. And the face of a former trick, apparently.

As Shane continues to spin gently in place, he sees something in the light fixture's glass leaves. It's them, he realizes. They're barely recognizable, and he can't tell if their faces are somehow being projected onto the glass folds or if the images emanate from within. But it's Cassidy and Andrew.

He's holding them in his hands. They haven't fallen. They haven't broken.

If there's a message to this impossible supernatural assault—*assault* seems like too strong a word given how gently he's being handled, but it's the first one that comes to mind—that must be it. He won't drop them. He won't break them. Some force he doesn't have a name for will support them, encircle them, and enfold them. All three of them.

The light fixture rises from his hands, swiftly but smoothly, as if it's being drawn upward by an invisible string.

Shane watches it pop back into place as smoothly as a button being snapped. As soon as his feet hit the floor, a wave of pleasure courses through him, so intense and powerful he has only seconds to pull his cock from his jeans before he empties his load onto the concrete floor.

He chokes back a cry he's sure will bring the entire restaurant outside to a halt if he lets loose. He's never cum like this in his life, jet after jet, never seen anything like it outside of porn films. And as it shoots from him, the vision he just beheld settles into his consciousness with surprising ease. If it was a ghost, was that its intention, to use pleasure to make Shane teachable and open?

You can have them both. Hallucination, spell, or haunting, whatever it was, that's the only meaning he can ascribe to it, to the delicate fixture balanced perfectly in his hands, and the faces of the two people he loves the most reflected in its crystalline folds. *Andrew and Cassidy. You can have them both and nothing will break.*

9

CASSIDY

The house is dark, save for the sparkling footprints dotting the foyer's hardwood floor. Gold flecks swim in each one, waterborne siblings of the luminescent particles that swirled through the candle's halo as soon as she lit the wick. They have to be Andrew's footprints, but she's shouted his name several times and he hasn't answered.

For the second time that day, Cassidy is soaked from head to toe and questioning the nature of reality.

The rain roused her after she lost consciousness. By then, the candle's glass container was completely empty, as if someone had wiped it clean of every last drop of wax while she'd drifted between sleep and waking, utterly drained by the most powerful orgasm she'd ever experienced.

LSD. Acid. Or maybe that Datura stuff Native Americans use for vision quests. Whatever it is, I'm still feeling it.

"Cassidy!"

She cries out. The front door is still open. Shane stands on the porch, soaked from head to toe. When she sees the tiny gold flakes dripping from his earlobes and the tip of his nose, pooling slightly in the hollows of his eyes, her breath leaves her.

Wide-eyed, his jaw tense, he closes the distance between them. He runs an index finger along her forearm and turns up a fingertip glistening with the same gold particles that highlight his face, that swim in the footprints all around them.

"What's going on?" Shane whispers.

"I don't know," she says, the rest of her sentence trailing off. It feels like a lie.

It *is* a lie. She accepted the invitation written on that note; that's what's happening. She lit Bastian Drake's candle at the scene of her greatest desire and now… and now…

Shane's lips are inches from hers. Rain swirls through the open door behind him. Flashes of lightning turn the branches outside into giant claws. But they don't frighten her. They do, however, seem to send a word of warning: *Stay inside. It's not safe to run. The answer, if there is one, is inside this house.*

"Andrew…" she whispers. "We have to find Andrew."

Shane follows her upstairs with bounding strides.

The master bedroom is empty. When she sees the alarm clock's blank screen, she realizes the power's out. She's about to scream her husband's name again when she sees him in the doorway. He is naked and dripping wet. Streaks of gold outline his nipples. They travel the hard ridges of his obliques and fringe the heft of his cock, which jerks from his sudden arousal. The sight of Cassidy and Shane standing together in the shadowed bedroom makes her husband instantly and powerfully hard. While it's too dark to see his face, she can see his muscular chest rising and falling with deep, sustained breaths. He always breathes like that when he's getting ready to pounce. To lick. To taste. To ravish.

"Get on the bed, Cassidy," he says, his voice low and deep.

Yes. Please. Now. If it's a mistake, I'll blame the candle. I'll blame Bastian Drake. But I want it now. Both of them. Here. Now.

In a flash of lightning, she sees Shane's expression. It's a portrait of astonishment and desire as he looks back and forth between the two of them. An expression just like the one he wore when he kissed her for the first time—not fear, but a kind of dazed wonder that life could suddenly deliver something so unexpected and all-consuming.

When Andrew grips the back of Shane's neck, this visual reminder of their moment at The Roquelaure House enflames her desire. Then her husband says, "Take your panties off, Cassidy," and it feels as if her skin has become a thin layer of radiant heat that can no longer contain the desire coursing through her veins.

Hands shaking, Cassidy unbuttons her skirt, kicks her way out of it. It turns into a brief struggle because she can't look away from what's happening in front of her. Bent at the waist, Shane runs his tongue up the side of Andrew's body, following a slender thread of gold all the way up to her husband's pecs. When he reaches Andrew's nipple, Shane sucks it briefly, loud enough to make a pop.

Her husband's low, throaty laugh is gentle. Shane's desire for Andrew is a feeling on Cassidy's skin as she peels off her bra and blouse, a tingly blanket. It feels like invisible hands have just lightly slapped her thighs, squeezed her breasts. As if she is being tweaked and teased and tested by the newness of what they're about to do, by the delicious danger of it. But there are no golden ghosts in the room with them now. It's just the three of them. And while everything about Shane's posture says he wants to suck her husband's tongue from in between his lips, Andrew teases him, gripping the back of his neck, holding their mouths inches apart.

"You're afraid, aren't you?" Andrew asks. "Both of you. You've always been afraid of how much you want each other. Afraid of how it doesn't fit into a neat little box." Their lips inches apart now, the two men she loves the most seem connected by a current of fearless desire, a current fueled by her exposed sex, by her wild passion for them both. "Well, *enough*! Both of you. Enough already. I've had enough of watching the two of you together."

His voice is a low growl and his wording makes her tense. If Andrew is about to punish them, why is he still stroking the back of Shane's neck? Why is he unbuckling Shane's belt with his other hand?

"All that hunger between you two, and it's got nowhere to go. Not anymore. 'Cause I'm gonna give it somewhere to go. I don't care if I have to fuck you both into loving each other the way you've always wanted to, always needed to. I'll do it. I'll do anything for you two, so why not this? Why not, huh? Get on your knees, Shane. It's time for you to taste my wife."

With a light pop, Andrew unbuttons Shane's pants from behind and slides them down his slender hips. All it takes to send Shane knees-first to the carpet is a light shove. Then Andrew sinks down behind him and starts steering him toward the foot of the bed, toward Cassidy's spread legs. He pulls Shane's rain soaked shirt over his head, revealing his lean torso, his perfectly etched abs, that blend of delicateness and hard edges that for years has held Cassidy in a kind of sustained swoon she has channeled into friendship. Her husband's muscular arms are a delicious contrast against Shane's smooth, pale skin. And while she might be the one sprawled on the bed, immobilized by anticipation and lust, they're the ones on their knees. They're the ones poised to worship her.

Her men. Finally. Both of them. *Her* men.

Dazed, Shane grips Cassidy's feet, one in each hand, squeezes them gently, as if he's trying to make sure they're real, that she's real, that *this* is real.

That afternoon she did her best to block out comes rushing back. They were watching television together when Shane suddenly ran one finger across the arch of her bare foot, and then suddenly he was tickling her furiously, and then just as suddenly he stopped, a hungry look in his eyes, as if he'd awakened something unexpected and powerful enough to carry them off in its grip.

I wasn't wrong. It wasn't just me. He could feel it, too. But we were so afraid, both of us. Because with just the two of us, it would never be possible. But it doesn't just have to be the two of us. It will never just be the two of us.

Andrew nuzzles his lips against the nape of Shane's neck, holds Shane in a vice-grip embrace from behind. But his eyes, like Shane's, are focused on her wet heat, even as he reaches down and starts to tug Shane's soaked underwear down over his ass. Shane's hands glide up her legs. His touch is hesitant at first. But then he adds pressure, exploring her. His fingers press down and revisit the places along her inner thighs that make her gasp and moan. Then they graze the edges of her pussy, teasingly. Again and again and again. Slow, matching circles of sweet torture on either side of her mound.

"Have you ever tasted a woman before, Shane?" Andrew asks with a devilish smile only she can see.

Don't, Andrew. Don't remind him he's never done this before just when he's about to finally—

"Yes," Shane answers.

What? When? If Shane's breaths weren't grazing her clit, she would probably bolt upright from shock.

"Superboy," Andrew says, "I thought we don't keep secrets from each other."

"We don't," Shane whispers. "Anymore."

And then, without a word of warning, her best friend's lips encircle her swollen nub. And as the pleasure arcs through her, she has a mad desire to say his name over and over and over again. She's said his name thousands, if not millions, of times before. She's shouted it across crowded restaurants. Barked it while laughing at one of his stupid jokes. But to say his name now, as he probes her with his tongue, would be to change the very nature of it, to change the nature of *him*, to change the nature of the two of them, together. Not just two of them, she realizes when she feels Andrew squeezing her thighs on either side of Shane's head. The three of them.

What starts as a gentle, hesitant nibble turns into a suckling that makes her cry out. Instinctively, she reaches for the back of his head, for that fine blond hair she's run her fingers through time and time again over the years, wondering each time what it would be like if the rules fell away, if labels ceased to exist. If they could have a moment like this. But before Cassidy can grip the back of Shane's head, Andrew grabs her wrist and firmly drives it to the comforter beside her. This is Andrew's lesson to give. For now, Andrew is in control. After all, he's the one who promised to set them free.

"Who was she?" Andrew asks, his voice thick with desire. He pulls Shane's mouth away from Cassidy's pussy. Shane's chin is lathered in her juices.

"No one. A client."

Jealousy, curiosity, and desire move through Cassidy in a swirl that curls her toes. Then her husband begins to lick her juices off of Shane's chin. His tongue finds Shane's. The two men meet in a passionate kiss, sharing the taste of her, and each other, for the first time. Her husband is more than just a director now. He's kissing another man—*with* her. *For* her. As hungry for the feel of Shane's lips as he is for the taste of her very essence.

"Just a client?" Andrew asks.

"And her husband," Shane whispers.

"At the same time?" Andrew asks.

It feels as if Andrew is reading her mind, asking the very questions she would ask if overwhelming desire hadn't rendered her voiceless and boneless.

"Yes," Shane whispers, and then he licks up her folds, finding her clit at the end with a mad flicker.

"And did you like it?"

"While it was happening, yes." Shane gasps. But he's staring down at Cassidy's wet heat, spreading her lips gently with both fingers, taking occasional, exploratory licks along the inside of her folds. Learning her.

Memorizing her. Worshiping her. "But when it was over," he says. *Lick. Lick. Breathe. Lick.* "All I wanted was you." With precision and care, he takes her swollen nub in between thumb and forefinger, rolls it gently, then looks up, studying her face, watching the delicious transformation each wave of pleasure sends through her expression. "*Both* of you."

"Shane..." *Don't ever stop. Don't ever leave. Don't ever be afraid again.*

"Both of you," Shane says again. "Always."

As Andrew's tongue travels the nape of Shane's neck, Shane stares into her eyes, hypnotized by the sight of her laid bare to him for the first time. When Andrew's fingers find Shane's hard, pink nipples, Shane shudders and sinks his teeth into his bottom lip. When Andrew gently sucks Shane's earlobe in his mouth, grips it gently between his teeth, Shane gasps. But even then, even as her husband's ministrations threaten to level him, Shane gazes into her eyes, never once breaking their connection.

She knows exactly what he's feeling, knows exactly the cascades of pleasure her husband can release with just his fingers and his tongue. For the first time, she's sharing this experience with the other man she can't live without, and it feels as if their souls have been unzipped from their bodies. As if the three of them are merging in the air above the bed like those golden ghosts that rose from Bastian Drake's candle.

"Cassidy," Andrew says.

"Yes, baby."

"Are you ready? Are you ready to feel Shane inside of you?"

"Yes..."

"Are you ready to watch the expression on his face when he feels how tight and hot you are? When he feels you clutching at him because you want him so badly? Because you've always wanted him?"

"Yes..."

"Are you ready to look into his eyes while you come?"

"Y-y—ye..."

With a devilish laugh, Andrew releases Shane from his embrace. Suddenly there's a loud crack followed by a sharp grunt. Her husband has just slapped Shane on the ass. Hard. Still shuddering from the delicious pain of Andrew's blow, Shane crawls up onto the bed, pressing down on her suddenly. The combination of submission and aggression coursing through his body makes her open for him like a flower.

"Cassidy..." he says, smoothing her hair from her forehead, lips grazing hers. Has her name ever carried so many meanings in a single utterance? She can hear Shane's astonishment that this is happening, his wonder at the feel and taste of her body. She can hear him asking her for permission. Permission to open her, to enter her. And because the answer is yes, she wraps her legs around his waist for the first time, and in response, his body arches against hers. This time, their kiss is pure abandon. The hesitancy is gone. The fear is gone.

Andrew rifles through the nightstand drawer. The sounds should be a distraction, but they're not. Because she knows exactly what he's looking for, the condoms they used for a while when she had to go off the pill because of some routine tests the doctor wanted her to have.

She's in such a rush to have him inside her she hasn't taken Shane's cock in her hand, hasn't explored him the way he's explored her. She grips it. Shane bites his lower lip, looks down, watches her stroke him with joyful disbelief. Each new touch, each new physical connection made for the first time is like another small tremor beneath that will shift the ground under their relationship forever.

"Wow. Not bad there, Superboy," she whispers.

And her teasing tone lights up his face with a broad smile.

"Want to know another secret?" Shane asks.

"*I* do," Andrew answers. Unwrapped condom in hand, he sinks down behind Shane, pulling him upright by one shoulder.

Once Andrew has righted him. The sight of Shane's dick sliding through her husband's powerful, veiny hands thickens the flow of her arousal.

"After I was with that woman," Shane says in between gasps. "You know, my client…"

"Yeah," she answers, but all she wants to do is kiss him, caress his face for the first time.

"I used to watch your face when you were laughing or eating dessert," Shane says. "I used to wonder if I could make you make those faces if I ever…"

"Fucked her?" Andrew asks. He tugs the condom down the last few inches.

"Or made love to her," Shane says softly, with a hint of childlike innocence.

"Yeah, well," Andrew says. He's got one arm wrapped around Shane's waist, but he's gazing down at her. They're both gazing at her. "I'll teach you how to do both."

Andrew leaps off the bed. The next thing she knows, he's sliding under her, hoisting her surrendered body up onto his, keeping her face up. His throbbing cock presses into the small of her back, his mouth finds the seats of pleasure along her neck, his hands knead her breasts, and his fingers find her nipples.

Shane is frozen, his sheathed cock hard and jerking in the air in front of him. When he senses their hesitation, Andrew draws one knee up in between Cassidy's thighs and uses it to open them further. Suddenly Shane's nose is grazing hers. Their lips are inches apart. He presses into her for the first time. Carefully. Gently. Reaching down and aiming with one hand. Never once breaking eye contact.

Once Shane is buried inside of her, Cassidy lets loose a series of wild sounds, unbidden and unrehearsed, only a few of them becoming words.

"Big..." she whispers. "Both of you...such big...boys."

"*Your* big boys," Andrew growls into her ear.

Shane starts to fuck her with long, slow strokes, allowing her to get used to the feel of him. Meanwhile, Andrew's fingers do a dance on her clit he's learned after years of memorizing the rhythms of her pleasure.

Over the course of their marriage, Andrew has taken her every which way from Sunday, but never quite like Shane is doing now; steady, determined, cupping her face in his hands, studying her, their lips grazing, each attempted kiss turning to gasps of pleasure. She has never cheated. For years it has been only Andrew, but now her body is being discovered again and by the man who already knows and loves every other part of her.

They work together. Her husband's hard body rocks up against her in time to Shane's strokes, his cock sliding teasingly in between the cheeks of her ass. For the first time in her life, pleasure feels like comfort, bliss like safety.

There's still a part of her that's convinced Shane might be faking the whole thing. So when he starts to grunt and pull away from her suddenly, she's afraid he might be flipping out. It doesn't even occur to her at first that it could be something else. Something far more obvious. He slides his condom off and unleashes his seed across her heaving stomach, grasping her shoulder for support. His mouth against her ear, Andrew says, "Yeah, yeah, yeah," over and over again. Encouraging, cheerful—the perfect director, the perfect coach.

And that does it. Together, Shane's pained sounding moans mingled with her husband's full-throated grunts of encouragement send the first wave of ecstasy arcing through her.

When she cries out, Shane cups the sides of her face, rests his nose against her nose, as if her orgasm were a shimmering, radiant thing from which he can draw more strength if they're as close as possible.

Andrew's hand slides between their stomachs, and then he slides a finger coated in Shane's cum in between Shane's lips. The debauched sight makes for a shuddering finish. She is wrapped in their heat and in their strength. Shane's body molds into hers. Andrew strokes her hair, then Shane's. Her shoulder, and then Shane's. He's in no rush to add his own orgasm to the mix but his groans are soft and satisfied too, as if he came as well. And for the first time in a long while, Cassidy is rendered silent by something besides fear, by the bliss of a dream realized.

"Belong to you," Shane whispers.

"Both of us, " she whispers back.

"*Always*," Andrew growls.

10

Cassidy awakens to the feel of Shane's breath against her collarbone and the delicious weight of Andrew's arm around her waist. The comforter slid off them during the night, leaving their entwined, naked bodies exposed to the morning sun. Daylight beats through the bedroom window, falling in a precise, accusing rectangle on their discarded clothes. Andrew usually draws the window shade at bedtime. But they slipped into unconsciousness as soon as Shane and Cassidy were leveled by their respective, toe-curling orgasms.

Were they truly exhausted, or was their sudden, deep sleep another result of the spell?

The spell. It's the first time she's used that word to describe Bastian Drake's candle, and it sends a bolt of fear through her.

A spell means it wasn't real. A spell means it was no different from being in a drunken blackout.

Slowly, she rights herself, gently lifting Andrew's arm off her waist. She scoots down the bed in between them. Only when she's free of the sheets does she look back to see if she awakened them by mistake.

Andrew stirs gently and takes Shane into his arms. By the time she's pulled her robe from the closet, her husband and her best friend are spooning. The sight of them together like this would have filled her with confusion and jealousy weeks before. Now it quiets her fears, fills her with a desire she no longer feels a desperate urge to contain or dismiss. The only thing she's wanted more than to be sandwiched between them, as she was last night, is to see them like this, their delicious physical contrasts entwined. It's as if her sun and her moon have met on the same horizon and their combined radiance is neither night nor day, but something almost otherworldly in its ferocity.

Maybe too *otherworldly. But if it were just a spell, wouldn't it have broken by now? Maybe this is*—her mind stutters before it gets to the word *real.* It happened; that's for sure. And it was good—dizzyingly, delightfully good. But if she's going to call it something *real,* that means something will have to come of it, something lasting. And the only way to tell if that's even a possibility is to find out just what the hell Bastian Drake put in that candle.

Halfway down the stairs she can tell the footprints that greeted her the night before are gone. There's not a single trace of gold residue anywhere on the hardwood floor.

How is that possible? Did they evaporate? Or did they disappear? She imagines them wafting up into the air like smoke while she and her two men slept upstairs. This vision sets her heart racing to fear's beat once again. If the spirits that literally moved the three of them to this place abandoned them this quickly, it doesn't exactly bode well for the future of this… What should she even call it? Threeway? Thruple? *Group possession?*

Belong to you…both of us…always. Were those last words the three of them whispered to each other before postcoital sleep the result of black magic? Her gut twists at the prospect.

Someone is coming down the stairs behind her.

For several seconds, she savors the uncertainty of not knowing if it's Andrew or Shane approaching her with quiet confidence, if it's Andrew or Shane sliding his arms around her waist, dipping his fingers under the flaps of her silk robe and caressing the skin underneath. Is it Shane or Andrew kissing her neck lightly, causing her to sway back and forth on her bare feet within the strong confines of his embrace?

"Are we glad or sad?" her husband whispers.

It's an old line that's turned into an old joke. When he was a teenager, Andrew's mother had been a self-help junkie, constantly modifying her parenting techniques in response to whatever faddish book on child rearing she'd read that week. At one point, she became so addicted to what she called "emotional temperature checks," she started greeting her kids every morning with the same question: *Are we glad or sad, dear?*

She turns to face him, and he takes her face in his hands quickly so he knows she's not trying to pull free, that what she really wants is to stare into his eyes, because her one-word answer requires all the bravery she can muster.

"Glad," she whispers.

"Good," he says with a smile. "Me too."

His lips meet hers. Their kiss is long, unhurried, his embrace so tight he's lifting her onto the balls of her feet.

"What'cha doing down here?" he finally asks.

"The footprints last night. You left gold footprints everywhere and I wanted to see if any were left."

"But they're not," he says.

"No. They're not."

"What does that mean?"

"I don't know yet. But someone does."

And it all comes out of her as she guides him to the living room sofa. She describes her visit to Bastian Drake's strange little shop, the candle with the invitation taped to its side. She keeps her voice to a whisper the entire time; the last thing she wants to do is wake Shane. If she's going to make any sense of last night's threeway, she needs to start by having a serious one-on-one with her husband.

"So you think we only did what we did because of this candle?" Andrew asks once she's finished.

"I think it had an effect, for sure."

"So you're afraid it's not real? You're afraid it was just a spell?"

"I don't know what it was. That's why I'm afraid. But what happened to you last night? Before, I mean. I saw the footprints when I got home, but what happened right before then?"

"I thought it was a hallucination, to be honest. It—*something* came out of one of the gas lanterns by the pool while I was swimming. It was a shape. I think it was a person. But if it was anything, it had to be a ghost."

"A ghost. And it came out of the flame, right?"

"Yeah. But, Cassidy, I don't think it was real. I think it was just a—"

"It's not possible for three people in three different places to have the same hallucination, Andrew."

"Well, we don't know what happened to Shane."

"Whatever it was, it made him come straight here. And his face was covered in the same gold stuff you tracked all over the floor, the same stuff that was all over my arms."

"Yeah. So?"

"*So?* Andrew, I have to find out what I did to you two. There might be long-term effects."

"Come on. It's not radiation, Cassidy."

"We don't know what it was, and we don't know what I did."

Andrew takes both of her hands in his, leans forward. There's a passionate gleam in his eyes, the same fire he gets when he's defending his political beliefs. For the first time since he's come downstairs, she takes in the fact that he's still naked; still beautifully, unabashedly naked. And still there, still *hers*, even after all the rules they broke together the night before.

"What you did, Cassidy," he says, "what *we* did was something we have wanted to do for years. When I fell in love with you, I fell in love with all of you—every part of you. And Shane is part of you. When the two of you are together you make something so beautiful I don't have words for it. And I've always wanted it."

"So you're in love with Shane, too?"

"It's not possible to be in love with you without being in love with Shane."

"Some people would say that's a bad thing."

"Yeah, well, not me. Maybe another man would have run from it. But the moment I first laid eyes on you together—remember? I'd been trying to find you for days after I met you in class, and then I finally tracked you down on the green, and the two of you…the two of you were…you were the most beautiful thing I'd ever seen."

Tell me his tears are real. Tell me he's not crying because of some damn spell.

"But you're not…gay?"

"Honey, you know the answer to that question," Andrew says, and then he slides a hand up her robe and caresses the inside of her thigh. "But I'm always happy to remind you."

"Is it like Danny?" she asks. "The way you feel about Shane?"

Andrew told her years ago about his only sexual experiences with another man, but they've rarely discussed it since then. She's afraid the mention of it now might send him reeling. But no, her husband appears utterly confident, utterly in control.

"Maybe," he says. "A little. My feelings for Danny…they happened over time. He was my best friend. I loved him so I wanted to make him happy. And it became more than that. It became a *desire* to make him happy. And that desire, well, my whole body responded to it. So yeah, maybe it's like what I feel for Shane now."

Or what Shane feels for me, she thinks. But her husband is still speaking so she gives him back her full attention.

"One thing's for sure," Andrew continues. "I've never looked at a man I didn't know and wanted to have sex with him. It's just not how I'm built. So who knows? Maybe I couldn't have done something like this when we all first met. But it's been years since then, Cassidy. Years of watching you two dance together at parties, years of listening to you two singing off-key to the same crappy songs on the radio."

"Why does it always get back to my taste in music?"

"Because you have really, *really* weird taste in music," he says, smiling. "But you know, Spice Girls aside, you're the most important person in my life, and Shane's the most important person in *our* lives. In the life you and I have together. Can't you see? For years we've been building this, and last night the final piece just fell into place. That's all."

When she doesn't respond, he slides across the sofa toward her, slipping behind her and taking her into his arms. It's similar to the reverse embrace he used to spread her open for Shane the night before. This fresh memory causes her head to spin, her breath to quicken. When the relaxing, narcotic effect of her husband's touch starts to wear off, she says, "I have to talk to him."

"Shane? We both do, I think."

"No. Bastian Drake. If that's even his real name."

"Maybe he's not real at all. Besides, it was just a note taped to the side of a candle. So what if you did what it said? How were you supposed to know what was going to happen?"

"His eyes."

"What?"

"His eyes. In the shop. When he was offering me the candle, when I wasn't going to take it, his eyes—they turned gold. Just like what you saw last night, just like what I saw. Pure gold. That's when I knew something... Part of me went into denial. I knew if I lit that candle at The Roquelaure House, something was going to happen. And I only did it because I was too afraid to come back here and talk about what we did during Mardi Gras."

"You were afraid to tell me how much you wanted it to happen again," he says.

It's not a question.

"Pretty much, yeah," she answers. "But still, the candle. I shouldn't have just—"

Andrew rights himself, cups her chin in one hand and draws her face to his. Their lips are inches apart, but his gaze is intent. "This is real, Cassidy," he whispers. "It's real. We're not here having this conversation because our heads were messed with by black magic. We did what we wanted to do. Didn't we? Wasn't it what you wanted?"

"Yes," she whispers. "But now that we've done it, I have got to make sure we're going to be okay." She kisses him quickly and slides off the sofa.

"Now?" Andrew asks. "You're going to talk to him now?"

"Yes."

"All right, well I'm going with you."

"No. You're staying right here."

"Why?" Andrew asks, dropping his voice to a whisper as he follows her up the stairs.

"As soon as he wakes up, Shane's going to freak. I need you to keep him from running. Do whatever it takes to keep him here."

"*Whatever* it takes?"

"Use your imagination if you have to."

Oh my God. Did I really suggest that?

Yes, you sure did. And if you keep thinking about it and don't start moving, you're going to end up in bed with them both again before you manage to track down Mr. Not-Your-Average-Candlemaker.

"How do you know he's going to run?" Andrew asks.

"He went missing for a week after the three of us made out for five minutes. Last night's gonna have him on the first plane to China."

"This was different, Cassidy."

They've reached the closed door to their bedroom.

"Trust me. He'll freak."

"Because he slept with a woman?"

"Because he slept with someone he has feelings for," Cassidy says. "*Two* someones. Look, Shane acts like he's this big player with no feelings. But that's only because he always keeps his feelings out of it. He never plays with anyone he actually cares about."

"And there's no one he cares about more than us."

"Maybe," she whispers, but everything inside of her yearns for this to be true, yearns to believe it with the same conviction Andrew does. She lifts Andrew's hand to her mouth, kisses the tips of his fingers. When she remembers the way he slid one of them in between Shane's lips the night before, her lips get tingly and her thighs flush. "Maybe," she says again, only this time it sounds more like a sigh.

"Cassidy, do you really think Bastian Drake is dangerous?"

"I don't think he's dangerous. I just don't think he's very direct when it comes to his product. And I have to know I didn't do something that's going to end up hurting the men I love."

At the sound of the panic in her voice, Andrew takes her in his arms again, brings his lips to her ear. "Well, I'm not feeling anything right now that feels like pain."

"An hour, maybe two," she says, returning his embrace. "If I'm not back by then, you and Shane can come down to the Quarter with guns blazing. Start on Dumaine Street between Burgundy and Dauphine. That's where his shop is, if it's still there. If I didn't imagine the whole damn thing."

Her husband's compliance is in his silence. But that's not enough. She takes his face in her hands, brings the tips of their noses together. "In the meantime, you do anything it takes to keep Shane from running again. *Anything.* And when I'm back, we'll figure this out."

"Two hours," Andrew says. "Two hours and then I'll call the cavalry."

"I don't think we're going to want to explain any of this to the *cavalry.*"

"I don't care who thinks I'm crazy. I just want you back safe."

He kisses her so forcefully her robe slips off her shoulders. She fights the urge to lift her legs off the floor and wrap them around his waist. She almost loses the battle; she's stroking one of his calves with her right heel, and her hands have turned to claws against the hard ridges of his back.

"Two hours," Andrew whispers.

He opens the bedroom door for her like an attentive valet.

Still tangled in the sheets, Shane doesn't wake up as she tiptoes toward her closet.

11

ANDREW

Andrew isn't sure caffeine will be the best thing for Shane's sure-to-be frayed nerves, but puttering around the kitchen beats hovering in the bedroom, waiting for him to wake up. Besides, he could use some coffee, too. It's his reward for managing to get through a quick shower without Shane sneaking out on him. He's only filled the coffee maker halfway when he hears footsteps on the stairs—pounding footsteps that come so fast it sounds like Shane will be out the front door in another few seconds if Andrew doesn't act right away.

In the foyer, he finds Shane struggling into his shirt while he spins in place, surveying the hardwood floor all around him.

"They're gone," Andrew says.

Shane whirls, wide-eyed. Did he think they'd left him?

"You're looking for the footprints, right?" Andrew asks. "She was looking for them too. But obviously they're not here anymore."

Maybe he won't be in such a rush to leave now that he sees Andrew was waiting for him to wake up.

Or maybe not.

When he takes in the sight of Andrew in only loose-fitting pajama bottoms, Shane blushes fiercely and turns his back to him. Then he punches his left arm through a dangling sleeve and starts buttoning up his jeans as he heads for the front door.

Damn. She was right. He's totally freaked.

"Shane…"

"I'm late," Shane says.

"For what?"

"Work!"

"Cassidy'll be back in an hour. Just hang out."

"I need to go. I've got an open house later."

"Open houses are on Sundays."

"I said *later*, didn't I? Sunday's later. Also, I'm going to drop in on my doctor and make sure I don't have a huge brain tumor that's making me see things."

"Quit being ridiculous."

"You're not a doctor."

"Shane, if it's a brain tumor that makes you see giant golden ghosts that give you amazing orgasms, then all three of us have the exact same tumor. And that doesn't seem very likely, does it?"

The part where giant gold ghosts gave them all great orgasms doesn't seem very likely either, but he keeps this to himself. Give Shane an inch of sarcasm and he'll take a mile, a mile that will have him out the door and out of his grasp.

Shane stares at him. He's managed to put himself together now, but it hasn't improved his mood.

"Ghosts?" Shane finally says. "Last night was about…*ghosts*?"

"Somewhat. I think… I mean, yeah. Sort of."

"Well, alrighty then. I guess that explains everything. Anyway, I'm going to work and if I'm not a blithering idiot by the end of the day, I'll talk to you guys later, after I've had about half a bottle of Grey Goose and maybe a Benadryl or two."

"Sit down, Shane."

"I'm not *sitting down*, Andrew," he says, gripping the knob. "Please. I just need to—"

Shane only manages to open the door a few inches before Andrew's on him. He throws his weight against Shane's, forcing him to shut the front door with his chest.

"Let me go," Shane says. But he whispers it the way he might whisper *Don't stop* or *Yeah, right there. That's the spot.* He paws weakly at the doorknob with his right hand, his eyes screwed shut, breathing hard and fast through flaring nostrils. Andrew can feel the gooseflesh his touch sends across Shane's skin.

"Jesus, " Andrew says. "You're really terrified, aren't you? She's right. When was the last time you had sex with someone you actually gave a shit about?"

"I'm not interested in being a prop to spice up someone's marriage."

"*Someone's* marriage? Quit being a dick."

"Quit making promises with yours you can't keep."

"What promises?"

"I can't, Andrew. I just... I can't."

"You can't what?"

"I can't just put on little shows with Cassidy to get you off. This isn't going to be a *thing* with us, okay?"

"I didn't get off, remember?"

"I'm not straight, Andrew. And I can't pretend to be for you or for her. Or for your viewing pleasure, or whatever last night *was*."

"You don't know what you are for Cassidy anymore and it's freaking you the fuck out. That's what last night was."

"Okay. Fine. So I'm a four on the Kinsey scale instead of a five. I admit it. Can I go?"

"I was there, dude. You're a three."

"Only when you're sucking on my neck. And I'd say that rounds me back up again."

This hoarse whisper—the blend of desire and anger in it—makes Andrew's balls tense up. "I promised Cassidy I wouldn't let you leave," he says in a voice that reminds him of his old football coach. "And I've never broken a promise to my wife. Not once."

"Just tell her I didn't feel like hanging out in the kitchen making small talk while we waited for her to come back and say this was all a mistake. A mistake with *ghosts*. So please, for the love of God, just—"

He pins Shane by his shoulder and slams his back against the door hard enough to rattle the frame.

"You little bitch," Andrew hisses.

Shane's blue eyes flare, maybe from pain, or maybe from shock that Andrew's mouth just closed over his. Andrew feels the shuddering effects of the tremulous thoughts ripping through Shane's mind. *Is this cheating? Should I fight? Can I fight?* Kissing Cassidy is like swimming in velvet. Kissing Shane is like rolling the tender sole of his foot gently back and forth over a tennis ball; a delicious, constant tug of war between tension and release.

"What are you doing?" Shane whispers.

"She said I had to do whatever I could to keep you here. So this is me, doing what I have to do," Andrew whispers. He starts to unbutton Shane's shirt before he realizes he doesn't have the patience for every single button. A tug on each flap and the thing pops open, buttons flying. Andrew brings his mouth to Shane's before Shane can look down and count how many buttons he just lost.

Once it feels like he's tongued the fight out of him, Andrew breaks and takes a deep breath.

"You really think I'm that easy?" Shane manages between gasps.

"Sure as hell feels like it," Andrew says.

A single, firm tug on Shane's unbuttoned jeans and Shane's absurdly hard cock bounces up into the air between them. In his rush to leave, Shane forgot to put on his underwear and now he is fully exposed.

With one arm braced across his chest, Andrew explores Shane's smoothness with his other hand, his fingers traveling to places he didn't touch the night before. When he gently traces the underside of Shane's hairless balls, Shane lets out a series of stuttering gasps. To hasten his surrender, Andrew sticks two of his fingers in Shane's lips, then, once they're slick with spit, he circles Shane's hole with them, triggering a wave of pleasure that makes Shane's legs go limp. To keep himself from collapsing, Shane slides an arm around Andrew's shoulders.

The smell of Cassidy's sex still blankets Shane's body, turning into a new and unnamed cologne Andrew can't resist. Andrew sinks to one knee, seizes Shane's cock by the root, runs his tongue down the length of it, tasting Cassidy. Tasting Shane. When he closes his mouth around the head, Shane yelps.

"You can't!"

"I can't *what?*" Andrew asks, standing until their lips are almost touching again. But he maintains his grip on Shane's cock, stroking him slowly and firmly.

Shane gasps, grits his teeth. "If it happens again… It has to be…"

"Has to be what, Superboy?"

"Both of you…always…"

"Interesting proposition," Andrew whispers. He finishes each stroke of Shane's shaft by gently kneading Shane's balls, then sliding his spit-slick fingers leisurely up and down the man's taint. Shane chews gently on his lower lip.

"No..." Shane whispers, but he sounds drunk, on the verge of blacking out from desire.

"No?"

"Won't work..."

"It's working now."

"You won't be able to handle the things I want to do to your body."

"Ha! I know a challenge when I hear one," he says.

Andrew releases Shane, who slides a few inches down the door, gasping, eyes glazed with lust. But there's regret on his face at being suddenly denied Andrew's touch. Andrew saunters into the living room, then, once he's sure he has Shane's undivided attention, he steps out of his pajama pants, one leg after the other, and tosses them aside.

"Prove it," Andrew says.

Shane is free now. Free to disappear for another week, or two, or three. Free to book himself a ticket on the first flight to China. Free to run, to ignore, to deny any of this ever happened. But the sight of Andrew's sculpted naked body, fiercely illuminated by the sunlight pouring through the front window, has Shane stumbling across the threshold to the living room, kicking himself out of his shoes and then his puddling jeans, until both men are standing several feet apart, stark naked, studying each other.

When Shane literally licks his lips, Andrew is surprised by a shiver of pleasure that travels from his balls all the way to his scalp. He's never offered himself to anyone quite like this. Never offered up his body so willingly, so submissively, and his heart races with as much fear as desire.

Not like Danny. This isn't like those times with Danny Sullivan at all. There's so much more here. So much more power. Danny and I were practically boys. But Shane is a—

"The minute you say no," Shane says with a new confidence in his voice. "The minute you resist, I walk out that door."

"All right—but no pain," Andrew says before he can stop himself.

"Some things only hurt for the first few minutes."

"Still, I'm not—"

"Relax. I won't fuck you until your wife asks me to."

Laid low beneath Shane's weight and his thrusts. Cassidy watching, directing. Like last night, only different players in different positions. Husband and wife reversed. Oh Jesus. Oh dear God. Could I? What am I doing?

No man has ever talked to him this way. With Danny, Andrew was always the aggressor, the dominant one. The only thing in play had been their mouths, maybe a finger or two. But the probing, penetrating fingers always belonged to Andrew. Andrew was always the one in control. But now…

Now Andrew is the one blushing, his breaths stunted, and Shane is the one with the wide, cocky grin on his face. Only once in his life has he felt this same blend of fear and arousal, and it was over a silly dream. When he and Cassidy first started dating, he had a nightmare that he walked in on her with one of his frat brothers, a nightmare so porny and vivid that when he woke from it he was gripping the pillow in jealous anger even as his cock throbbed against the sheets.

"Are you done whining?" Shane asks him.

"Are you done running your mouth?"

"You only get to set one limit today and you just did. Say no, try to stop me from doing anything else, and I'm out the door and you get to explain to Cassidy how you weren't man enough to finish what you started."

"Deal."

Shane points toward the sofa. "Sit," he orders.

But Andrew doesn't sit. Instead, Andrew kneels on the sofa cushions, pitches forward and grips the back of the sofa in both hands, sticking his bare ass out into the air behind him. He gives it a little wiggle for good measure. No way is he giving up all the control. Besides, Shane's probably so hungry for his cock, he won't be able to keep up the dominant routine for long.

"Oh, I see," Shane says, in response to Andrew's small act of defiance.

Now he'll have to flip Andrew over. Now he'll have to show how much he's really hungering for Andrew's dick. And man, he should pull the window shade because if someone comes up the front walk, they're totally going to be able to see us.

"Shane."

It feels like the pleasure sweeping through him suddenly is trapped inside a shell of panic and riding a tide of incredible, unexpected vulnerability. If the shell cracks and the emotions are set free, he'll cross over into some new realm of previously unknown bliss. But part of him can't help but fight it because it feels wrong. Beyond wrong. Beyond forbidden. He didn't know he had so many nerves down there, didn't know they could be used against him this way. Against his ego, his aggression, his masculinity. The gasps and moans coming from him sound genderless and desperate. Andrew reaches behind him, grabbing for Shane's head. But Shane bats his hands away with one swift strike.

"Remember the rules?"

"But wait, stop—you c-can't—"

"Oh, *what?* You thought you could take a little control back? Make me repeat my instructions? Make me beg for your cock? Is that it?"

"Seriously, Shane. You have to sto— You have to..." *Lick. Probe. Lick. Bite. Slap.*

"I tell you to sit and instead you wiggle your hard ass at me like a cock tease, *after* you told me I couldn't fuck it? Well, this is what you get for that, Mr. Burke." Mr. Burke is what Cassidy always calls him when she drags him into the bedroom for some naughty, late-afternoon role-play. Hearing it out of Shane's mouth makes him wonder how many details of their sexual adventures she's shared with Shane, and how many of those details have fueled Shane's appetite for him. The thought of them together, discussing his body, discussing the tender, special spots on his skin, makes him dizzy with desire.

"I can't be—I mean, you have to st-stop or I..."

Shane smacks his lips and draws his mouth from Andrew's ass. "*This* wasn't the limit!"

"Still I..."

Andrew can't speak, because even his mind can't fasten on the words for what Shane is doing. *Shane's mouth, down there. Can't see. Is it just his mouth? Is it his hand? No. His hands are on my cock, on my balls, so it has to be just his— Fuckfuckfuckfuck*fuck... His thoughts spill out into frenzied gasps.

"Fuckfuckfuckfuckfuck—"

"I thought *that* was your limit," Shane growls. Then he goes back to work, his flickering tongue fearlessly traveling the sensitive, unexplored crack of Andrew's ass.

Just like it traveled Cassidy's wet, throbbing cunt. The same tongue, the same flickering motions. The same ravenous hunger.

And the hard shell encasing the pleasure rocketing through him cracks.

Oh, God. Is this what she feels when I taste her, when I lap at her juices? Is this some sense of the bliss she felt as Shane devoured her lips, her folds, her hard little clit?

Miraculously, he's been joined with the waves of pleasure he saw coursing through his wife the night before, all thanks to Shane's skillful, fearless tongue. This realization unleashes something inside of him. His mouth opens against the back of the sofa. The cry that rips from him is as abandon-filled as the one he let loose in the swimming pool the night before. Only now there are no ghosts, no visions, just Shane's unleashed appetite, his ravenous worship of Andrew's body. *Every* part of Andrew's body. Shane's hand strokes Andrew's cock, suckles Andrew's balls, and travels places he's never allowed Cassidy to fully explore.

Two desires fill Andrew—to take Shane into his arms and hold him as tightly as he can, and to fuck him senseless on the living room floor, as hard as Shane fucked Cassidy the night before. While it feels like they should be competing for control—these wild desires—they join with each other instead, forming an overwhelming river of desire that leaves him submissive, gasping and exposed; powerless with hunger under Shane's forbidden, oral assault.

When Shane rolls him over onto his back, Andrew is rag-doll limp, entirely at the mercy of Shane's maneuvering grip on his thighs.

Now he can watch Shane work.

Cassidy knows how to make him feel like a stud, knows the words and phrases that will set him off, knows how to run her hands over his body like he's a statue in a museum come to life and she's the last lustful security guard on duty. But Shane's combination of aggression and worship is a new experience, and it feels as if every cell in Andrew's body is realigning itself to accept Shane's blazing, unexpected gifts.

Dominating Cassidy and Shane together, forcing them to unleash their conflicted desires for one another, has always been his fantasy. But never did Andrew think Shane—his mouth, his ferocity, his beautiful blue eyes and his slender, hard body—could also allow him to experience the same pleasures that ricochet through Cassidy in the bedroom.

Shane sucks him with practiced skill, his tongue flickering across the front of his corona in just the right spot. *He knows just how to do this, how to do me. Because Cassidy told him. Cassidy shared with him every secret of my skin.* He feels bathed in their mutual desire, and this brings him to the edge.

Shane lets out a sharp, satisfied groan at the taste of Andrew's fresh flow of arousal.

"Shane…"

"Give it to me," Shane whispers, unwilling to draw his mouth more than an inch or two off Andrew's cock as he strokes him furiously.

"Shane…"

"All of it, Andrew. Every drop."

It's an order, a command. The feverish spasms of pleasure that await Andrew will lay him open, he's sure of it; Shane must sense this as much as Andrew does. Shane must know Andrew has never come in anyone else's mouth before, anyone besides Cassidy. Not even the women he was with before they met, or Danny Sulliva—

Andrew screams. He'd love to believe it was really a yell or a war-whoop or a bellowing cry. But it wasn't any of those things. It was a scream. His entire body spasms, his legs kicking up on either side of Shane's head, his back rearing up off the sofa cushions, his abs tensing so hard spikes of pain shoot through him, all while his seed gushes into Shane's mouth. Amidst this wordless pleasure is a fear, a fear that this is the strongest orgasm he's ever had in his life, and it's happening with a man, and does that mean he might be more into guys than he's ever—and then Shane withdraws the finger he deftly slid inside of Andrew's hole, releases the pressure he applied to his prostrate at just the right moment, and Andrew starts to laugh.

Maybe it was the strongest orgasm I've ever had because no one's ever stuck a finger up my ass before.

Slowly, Shane draws his mouth from the root of Andrew's cock, all the way up its length, until the head pops free of his slick, pink lips. He gazes into Andrew's eyes. Andrew can't believe what he's seeing, so he reaches out for Shane's chin, his cheeks, checking to make sure Shane actually swallowed every drop, that none of it is smeared across his face.

After a few minutes of this, Shane reaches up and takes one of Andrew's fingers into his mouth, suckles it gently, as if whatever he tastes on it is quieting his heart, relieving him of the need to come.

"So…" Andrew tries, but his voice is hoarse and he has to clear his throat. "You fucked me without fucking me."

"Yeah," Shane answers, still biting down lightly on Andrew's fingertip.

"So how'd I do? Did I pass my test?"

"It was a good start," Shane whispers.

"Not good enough to make you come."

"I'm saving it for later."

"For Cassidy?"

"For both of you," Shane answers, then he kisses Andrew's fingertip.

Shane goes to stand, and Andrew tugs on his hand. "No," he says.

"I just need to go to the bathroom."

Andrew swings his legs up onto the sofa, pulling Shane down onto the space he's just opened up on the cushions. "You need to stay right here until Cassidy gets back."

"I won't leave," Shane says. "I promise."

"Only one way to be sure," Andrew answers.

Shane plops down on the edge of the sofa, studying Andrew over one shoulder.

Amazing. Just swallowed every last drop of my cum and he's still afraid to snuggle with me.

"Lie down," Andrew says quietly. "I passed my test, now it's time to pass yours."

"I thought last night was my test."

"Nope. There are all kinds of ways to run, Shane. You don't always have to use the front door."

"Ha! So you're a cuddler?" Shane asks. "I had no idea."

"You had *every* idea," Andrew answers. "Admit it. Cassidy's told you everything about me. How else would you know *exactly* how to suck my cock?"

"Experience. Intuition."

"Lie with me, smart mouth," Andrew says.

His breath leaving him in a long, dramatic sigh, Shane sinks down onto the narrow band of cushions in front of Andrew, snuggling into Andrew's chest.

"See. That's not so bad, is it?" He slides an arm over Shane, gradually tightening his grip around his stomach.

"Uh-huh."

"This way, you can't pretend I'm some random guy you picked up in a bar. This way you can accept that this is real. That it's really happening." He kisses Shane's earlobe, then his neck, gently, careful not to arouse too much desire.

In the sudden silence between them, Andrew hears the sudden patter of rain followed by a neighbor's car backing out of a nearby driveway; it reminds him they just conducted a debauched scene in the middle of the living room. On a weekday morning no less!

Shane's breaths are slow and steady. Andrew wonders if the guy's on the verge of passing out again. Then he speaks. "Fine," Shane says. "This is really happening."

"Yep."

"Is it going to happen again?"

"I hope so."

"Me, too. So we're just going to lie here like this until Cassidy comes home?"

"I gave her two hours. She's got one left. But, yeah, that's my plan."

"You have a lot of plans, Andrew."

"I'm an architect."

"You don't think she'll freak out when she sees us like this?"

"Are you kidding? She practically set this whole thing up. Also, have you seen the gay porn on her laptop?"

"Seriously? I *gave* her that porn, Andrew. She said she wasn't a fan. She said the guys were hot, but there wasn't enough of a *story*."

"Guess that's our job then."

"To make her some porn?"

"No. To give her a story."

"I see. You think she'll be okay that you and I…"

"I was okay with you two last night, wasn't I?"

"That was different. You wanted us together."

"If you think she doesn't want us together, then you haven't been paying attention for years now."

In the silence that follows, he expects Shane to dispute this, or at the very least fire up some of his usual snark. "I have been," he says instead. "I have been paying attention. I just didn't think it was possible."

"It is," Andrew answers. "It is possible."

Instead of responding, Shane clasps one of Andrew's hands tightly to his sweaty chest.

"First she's got to figure out what the deal is with that candle, though," Andrew says.

Shane rolls over until their noses are almost touching, looking genuinely confused.

"What *candle?*" he asks.

12

CASSIDY

Closed.

The other stores around the courtyard are open for business, but this small, bluntly worded sign hangs inside the glass front door of *Feu de Coeur*. The shop is so dark there's barely enough light to reflect off the glass containers lining its front window. From a few feet away, it's impossible to tell they hold candles.

Closed? That's all? At the very least, she expected a handwritten sign with calligraphic script saying, *I shall return shortly—Bastian.* Or maybe a miniature clock with plastic arms set to the time the store will open again.

Unsure of her next move, she wanders back out onto Dumaine Street and flips up the hood on the raincoat she found in her trunk.

Lord. Enough already with this damn rai—

—and the rain stops.

She is staring down at the sidewalk in a daze when it happens. The quality of the sunlight changes suddenly. It isn't darker or brighter—it's different. Because the rain didn't just stop, it *froze*. The milky gray light of a cloud-filled sky is now reflected through a thousand suspended crystals of water. The silence is sudden and total. A forest of frozen droplets stretches out on all sides of her.

If it hadn't been for the night before, she would probably be in hysterics right now, curled in a ball on the sidewalk, asking God if she had died. But instead, she reaches into the air in front of her and watches her hand move through the drops as if they weren't even there. And then, through the impossible silence, comes the sound of footsteps.

He's about half a block away, dressed much as he was the day before. A vest of dark brown silk, rather than purple, trousers pressed with a knife's edge, polished brown loafers without a spot of rain on them. The umbrella must be for show, given that he doesn't have a drop of water on him. Indeed, water doesn't seem to touch this man at all; like when he took the wet rolls of tapestry from her arms yesterday without getting a stain anywhere on his clothes. But still, Bastian Drake makes a show of lowering the umbrella to his side, closing it with a soft click, and resting the tip on the sidewalk next to him, Charlie Chaplin style.

"I trust everything went well?" he asks.

"Was it a spell, Mr. Drake?"

"Call me Bastian."

"Is it your real name?"

"It's been my name for eighty-six years, so it might as well be."

"And before that?"

He smiles and studies the street scene around them as if it were just another spring morning.

"Are you a vampire?" she asks him.

"Oh, *vampires*. Please. I can't stand the sight of blood. And besides, they're not *real*."

"But you're real. *This* is real. Can other people…can they *see* this?"

"Only the ones who have enjoyed my gift to its fullest potential."

He's just given her enough information for her mind to grab on to. Her quick calculations tow her from a swamp of confusion.

His name's been Bastian Drake for eighty-six years, but he doesn't look a day over thirty-five. He's a ghost; he has to be. So he must have died at thirty-five, but when he was alive he probably had a different name. Since then he's been frozen in time. And apparently he can freeze time too, which isn't something she's ever associated with ghosts. But it's not like she majored in Ghost Studies in college.

There's a car frozen halfway through the intersection a block away, its windshield wipers arrested in mid-swipe, the driver an indecipherable blur through the crystalline forest. "Is this the same thing you did last night?" she asks.

"Oh, no. Not at all. And I didn't do anything last night, Cassidy."

"Your candle sure did."

"The candle gave you a nudge, that's all."

"Eight-foot-tall ghosts? Spontaneous orgasms? That's quite a nudge."

"It's quite encouraging, isn't it? But still, nothing about it deprived you of your free will."

"So it wasn't forced on us?"

"Did it feel as if it was?"

"I guess not. But what if we'd just freaked? I mean, what if I never went home last night? What if I'd gotten in my car and just kept driving?"

Bastian Drake's smile flickers before it fades altogether. When he speaks again, it's in a more clipped and quiet tone than any he's used with her since they met. "Best not to meditate on the road not taken, Cassidy."

A far cry from what he said to her in his shop the day before. She struggles to remember the words he used. *Take it from a man who passed up far too many gifts in his life. There is no virtue in ignoring your heart's desire. To ignore it is to condemn yourself to a lifetime of darkness.* Even though she's not sure exactly who or what he is, she's willing to bet most of Bastian Drake's existence is spent meditating on the road he didn't take. What else could he have meant by a *lifetime of darkness*?

"That sounds scary," she says.

"All three of you chose to embrace the flame. This is a good thing, Cassidy. When the flame is not embraced, there are consequences for everyone involved."

"I see. So this is what you do with your magic? You help people live out their fantasies?"

"The fantasies that guide them to their hearts, yes."

"I see. And the ghosts we saw last night. Who were they?"

"Well, for starters, they weren't ghosts."

"But you are," she says quickly.

"Clever," he whispers.

"Thank you. So last night?"

"Have you ever heard mention of a place called The Desire Exchange?"

Sure, she wants to say as a chill moves through her. *I've also heard of Bigfoot, alien abduction conspiracies, and all manner of creepy stuff I probably would have laughed off a day ago.* "It's a sex club for rich people out in the swamp somewhere," she replies. "But I don't know anyone who's actually been. It's an urban legend, a myth."

"Ghosts who can stop time are also a myth, Cassidy. But you're speaking to one of them right now."

At least you finally told me what you are.

"Okay. So The Desire Exchange is real. But what does it have to do with the candle you gave me?"

"The Exchange is a place for people to live out their deepest sexual fantasies. Most people visit in the hope of discovering if it's just a fantasy or a calling they've always ignored. A calling that could turn into a new beginning. But many of them learn they need only act it out once and then they're free of it. For these people, it's more of a purge. Either way, the passion and bravery of those who visit The Desire Exchange gives off a kind of energy. I bottle that energy, I blend it, and I place it on a shelf where it waits for someone like you, someone who could use a bit of inspiration."

"Inspiration?"

"A nudge," he says with a bright smile. "Don't worry. This isn't the beginning of a haunting. What you saw last night will never come again. It's up to you to shape your story now. You and Andrew and Shane."

"Just tell me you're not stealing people's souls."

"Oh, for goodness sake! No. What is with this *incessant* belief that the dead want only to hurt the living? It's the great misconception of the plane on which you dwell. The engine of the living world is *love*, Cassidy. Not money. Not pain. Not war. Love. And there are those of us who are senten—there are those of us who are *assigned* to make sure the engine keeps running."

Sentenced. You were going to say sentenced, *not assigned.*

"So last night, those things. If they weren't ghosts, what were they? *Who* were they?"

"*They* are still very much alive, so you needn't worry about them. All you saw was their essence, the life force that sprang from their passion and their desire."

"A woman and two men. Just like me, Andrew, and Shane?"

"Exactly," Bastian answers with a satisfied smile.

"Did it work out? Did the three of them end up together? Or did they just live it out once so they could purge it and move on with their lives?"

"Their story is not mine to tell."

"What about my story?"

"Not just *your* story, Cassidy."

"Sorry. *Our* story. Me and Andrew and Shane."

"Is yours to live," he says.

"But what if—"

"*What*, Cassidy? If you give into fear again? If you refuse to admit that you love them both equally, that you always have, that you've longed for a special sacred place where all three of you could be together, always? Are those the *what ifs* you can't bring yourself to name?"

Belong to you…both of you…always. If she's being haunted by anything right now, it's these words, the words they whispered to each other before they fell asleep in each other's arms. Her heart won't rest until they've spoken these words to each other again, without the sparkling evidence of Bastian Drake's magic threaded across their bodies.

"We can't light one of your candles every time we want to be together," she says. "That's not going to work, is it?"

"You are correct. My gift has done its job. The rest is up to you now."

A gold radiance has returned to Bastian's eyes. This time Cassidy doesn't turn away from the magic in front of her.

She has what she came for, Bastian's assurance that if there are battles lying in wait for her, and for Andrew and for Shane, those battles will pit them against their own hearts, not dangerous spirits. But still, she could stand here all day questioning him. And somewhere along the way, she would probably ruin the whole thing. By the hundredth question, her head would take control of her heart and she would analyze the source of this miracle in such microscopic detail she'd convince herself it was all just a bunch of strange chemicals damaging brain cells, making them misfire.

Also, it seems like Bastian Drake is done with their little chat.

There's a crackling sound all around them, as if the frozen tableau they're standing in the middle of is actually an ice palace that's started melting in the sun. She figures this is Bastian's not-so-subtle warning that he's about to release his hold on the clock of human time. That, combined with the gold radiance that's chased the pupils from the man's eyes, convinces her she doesn't have much time left with him. And maybe he's pulling back for the same reason she believes she should. Maybe he's sensed that the more she discusses his magic, the more she'll wipe its gold dust from her heart. So as the crackling sound around them intensifies, Cassidy says the first words that come into her head.

"Thank you."

Bastian Drake smiles, and then suddenly falling rain wipes him from view.

13

CASSIDY

"Hey," Cassidy says.

"Howdy," Shane answers.

It takes her a few seconds to realize Andrew has handcuffed Shane to the bedframe with a set of fuzzy handcuffs he's only used on her once or twice, maybe because she's a bigger fan of silk wrist ties. The running shower in the master bathroom makes a dull roar.

When she takes a seat on the bed beside Shane, she sees his skin is still rosy from the shower and scented with her husband's favorite peppermint body wash. He's dressed in her husband's clothes too; a pair of his plaid Ralph Lauren boxer shorts and one of the white tank tops he likes to wear to bed.

"How'd you shower in those?" she asks.

"He put them on me after. But he stood guard the whole time so I couldn't get away."

"And did you want to get away?"

"Well, see, he told me this woman I love more than anything went and did something really dangerous all by herself. So I freaked out. I said we had to find her. But he had other ideas. Something about keeping a promise to his wife. That's been the big theme this morning, keeping promises to Cassidy Burke."

"So what was this dangerous thing this woman went and did?"

"She had a meeting with some guy named Bastian Drake."

"Yeah, well, turns out he's not dangerous."

"Okay, fine. But see, this woman, she didn't know that before she went down there, *alone*, did she?"

"Uh-huh. Well, if someone hadn't been ignoring my text messages for a week, I might not have ended up in his shop in the first place."

"*Oh my God. So* not fair, Cass," he says, dropping the sly routine.

"I know. And it might not be all that true, either."

"What do you mean?"

"Apparently his candles find exactly who they need to find. That's how it works. I probably would have smelled it from halfway across the city."

"What did it smell like? The first time?"

"You," she says, staring into his eyes. "You and Andrew, together."

He blushes—god, he's so cute when he blushes. She's always thought so but she's never been able to say so without feeling like a desperate, pathetic, deluded woman hopelessly in love with her gay friend. She expects him to look away from her penetrating stare, but instead he nibbles on his lower lip, meets her stare and asks, "Did I smell good?"

"Very," she answers.

"Have I always smelled good?"

With one bare foot, he drags his toes gently across her bent knee. His cock is starting to rise in the loose folds of her husband's boxer shorts, and she wonders if it's the result of being cuffed, asking her coy questions, the lustful stare she's giving him or all three in combination.

"Yes," she answers.

He slides his foot up onto her leg, and once the bare sole is exposed, she realizes what he's doing, referencing that little moment they shared together, a moment of such unexpected, flowering desire she barely managed to repress her memory of it until they made love the night before. She drags one fingertip along the arch of his foot, and he sucks in a breath through clenched teeth.

"So what did you and my husband get up to while I was gone?"

"Do you want me to tell you?" he asks her. "Or do you want me to show you?"

Her heart races. She grasps Shane's bare foot in one hand. His perfectly manicured, pale foot. Just then, the shower shuts off. A minute later, Andrew appears in the doorway, toweling himself off, trying to appear relaxed and casual even though he's clearly dying for information about her trip to the French Quarter. The sight of them touching brings a smile to Andrew's face.

The smile fades when she starts to recount everything Bastian told her, including a description of the frozen rain that leaves both Andrew and Shane speechless. By the time she's done, Shane is sagging against his handcuffs, and Andrew is wrapping his towel snugly around his waist.

After a few minutes of silence, her husband takes a seat on the foot of the bed, his back to them, as if he needs to stare at the carpet to absorb everything she just described. "Y'all remember my aunt Linda?"

"Of course," Cassidy answers. "She couldn't stand me."

"She called me the *gay one*," Shane says.

"Exactly. You remember how uptight she was, how everything in her house was always perfect. Totally straightlaced, super conservative. Church every Sunday."

"We remember," Cassidy says.

"A few years before she died, she had too much to drink one night. I mean, it was, like, the *only* night I ever saw her have too much to drink. And she told me this story. She was walking her dog out at her husband's fishing camp and this little girl ran across the trail right in front of her, chasing this red plastic ball. There wasn't another house within ten miles, not so much as an access road near the trail. All around was just swamp. Anyway, as soon as Linda tried to run after her, the girl just disappeared. When she got back to camp, she called the cops, described the girl to them, just to, you know, see if there were any missing person reports for a child who matched that description."

"And?" Shane asks.

"There was just one report from the year before. For a girl who eventually turned up dead because her father killed her."

"*Aunt Linda* told you this story?" Cassidy asks.

"That's what I'm saying. She wasn't exactly a tarot card reader. Never read a scary book, never watched scary movies. She wasn't someone who *wanted* to believe in anything except the Lord. But she saw something she couldn't explain and she kept it a secret for most of her life. Ever since the night she told me, well… I told myself a time would come. That something might happen to me too. Something that would change what I believed was possible."

"So you don't think we're hallucinating anymore?" Cassidy asks.

"I didn't think it this morning. I just didn't want you to leave, babe. Anyway, what I'm trying to say is, I think everybody has their Aunt Linda moment eventually. I'm just glad I'm not having mine alone."

"Me, too," Cassidy says.

"Me, three," Shane answers.

"But they weren't ghosts," Cassidy says.

"I hope not," Shane answers. "'Cause I knew one of them."

Andrew turns so quickly at this announcement, the towel slips free of his waist. Cassidy is stunned, waiting for Shane to say he's kidding. But Shane stares back at them intently, nodding.

"I was in the bathroom at Perry's when it happened," he says. "Samantha and I were having dinner. I looked up and there was this golden…*man* staring back at me from the mirror. And it was Jonathan Claiborne."

"The guy you hooked up with?" Cassidy asks. "The waiter?"

"He's not a waiter anymore apparently, but yeah, Samantha and I'd been talking about him before I got up from the table, so I thought it was…you know, I thought I was hallucinating."

"Maybe you were," Andrew says. "I mean maybe the *ghost* was real, but his face was vague and you just filled in the gaps."

"It's possible. I don't know. But you want to know the other thing?"

"Yes," Cassidy says.

"I don't care," Shane whispers. He's looking back and forth between the two of them. When he speaks again, his voice has a catch in it, a catch that brings Cassidy's hand to his knee. "I don't care why we did it. I don't care if it was ghosts or magic or drugs. All I know is that I don't want it to end. I never want it to end. In high school, whenever I looked at a beautiful guy, I would feel this sadness, like this heaviness in my heart. Because I didn't want to be attracted to men. I didn't want to find men beautiful. And then I came out and I was Mister Proud Gay Man and the sadness went away, for a while, at least. But then, a few years ago, it came back. It came back whenever I looked at the two of you together. And that's when I knew I wanted you both, but I thought I could never have you."

Andrew stands up suddenly. What is he doing? Is he about to leave?

"Babe…" Cassidy says.

"I think," Andrew says. "I've made my case to both of you. And quite well, I might add. So at this point, if there's anything standing in the way of this, it's going to be between the two of you. So I'll give you all some time alone."

"Kind of like the time you two had alone this morning," Cassidy says.

"Kinda, yeah," Andrew says with a grin. "Shane here's afraid he's only a four on the Kinsey scale unless I'm chewing on his neck. Given what I saw him do to your body last night, I don't really think that's true. But it doesn't matter what I think. It matters what he thinks. And what you think." Andrew rounds the foot of the bed and gives her a lingering kiss. "So convince him."

His hand reaches for hers. She looks down in time to see him place the key to the handcuffs in her open palm.

It feels like she's about to get away with something. Something her husband just gave her permission to get away with. The door clicks shut behind Andrew, and they're left alone. She's too nervous to look into his eyes. She gets up on her knees and slides the key into the handcuffs.

"Don't." His voice is as tight as a drawstring.

Her heart drops. Is this where it ends? Is the convincing part already over with? Is the prospect of being left alone with her body too terrifying for him to face? When she summons the courage to look down at him, dread swirling in her stomach, she sees Shane's eyes are hooded with desire.

"Don't uncuff me, Cassidy."

The key shakes in her hand.

"Don't let me go," he whispers.

"Shane…"

"Touch me everywhere you've always wanted to," he whispers. "Don't ask for permission. Own me, Cassidy. Own me like you always have."

Her urge is to tear his clothes off, to emulate the way Andrew ravishes her. But that's not the invitation he's extended. Owning him will mean *her* pace, *her* urges and desires. She takes her time pulling the boxers down his smooth thighs, grazing his cock with her fingers. Tickling it. Nibbling the head slightly. No shoving his cock down her throat in some mad rush to deep-throat him to orgasm. Instead, she learns the map of his sensitive spots.

He's told her about some of his special places over the years, but she's unprepared for the cry that rips from him when she pushes his tank top up over his chest, secures one nipple gently between her teeth and flickers her tongue over it, or the near hysterical giggles that rip through him when she teases the edges of his armpits with her fingers.

Every step of the way, she feels a nagging urge to be more aggressive, more masculine. But each time she feels it, she pulls back, reminding herself of his offer.

Own me...

It is her gentle touches and tastes and scratches that push Shane to the brink of ecstasy. Maybe because they're new and unfamiliar, a barrage of delicious shocks to his system. When she drags the fingernails of one hand down the sides of his body, he screams as if he's been penetrated. His throbbing cock jumps against his flat, hairless stomach. She repeats the motions back and forth, just her fingernails, up and down that pale, hairless torso.

"Cassidy!" She ignores the breathless, pleading urgency in his tone, drags her fingernails further down his body, across his hips, down the insides of his thighs. When his hips rise up off the bed, she gives in to temptation, grasps the base of his cock, and slides it down her throat.

His lips part. He's sucking air, trying to make words. "Give me... Let me..." It takes her a moment to realize what he's asking for. Her urge is to let him undress her, but that would mean surrendering her control. Standing over him, she pulls her shirt off, unsnaps her bra. His mouth opens when her breasts are still inches away. As soon as she hits her knees next to the bed, he bucks his head off the pillow, snags her nipple in between his lips, and tongues the sensitive nub. To keep from going over, she grabs the bedframe in one hand, right above the spot where Shane's wrists buck inside the padded handcuffs.

"You like that?" she asks. Her voice sounds like another woman's.

"Give me the other one," he answers with a devilish grin. "Just so we can be sure."

"Bad boy," she whispers.

"Very, very bad boy. Now give me the other one. *Please.*"

"Hey. I thought I'm in charge here."

"Oh, I'm sorry, Mrs. Burke. Is there something you'd like more?"

He swirls his tongue across her nipple, gazing up into her eyes. Those big beautiful blue eyes. For years, she's stared into them for comfort and solace, and now they provide her with something altogether different— pure pleasure.

When she straddles him, he bites the edge of her panties, peels them off her mound just enough that he can begin working his tongue into her folds. The desperate hunger of this frenzied probing has her gripping the bedframe in one hand, peeling the lace to one side with the other hand, giving him full access. Then she rides his mouth, watching his wrists move against the padded handcuffs. She's so lost in the bliss of it, she doesn't hear Andrew approaching, doesn't see her husband until he's slipped the keys to the cuffs inside the lock. The minute he frees Shane's hands they fly to Cassidy's thighs, gripping and pulling so he can angle himself more precisely against her clit. Even with his hands free, he is still her worshipful slave.

Andrew cups her chin in one hand, brings his mouth to hers. She returns his kiss as best she can, even though Shane's hungry ministrations leave her gasping. Andrew is hard as a rock as he turns to dig in the nightstand drawer with one hand.

A defiant, willful part of her mind assesses each swipe of Shane's tongue across her pussy for any sign of resistance, but it doesn't find any. Even if there's some part of Shane that will always be purely, resolutely homosexual, it's being overpowered by a thundering need to give her overwhelming pleasure. These thoughts have her ablaze. Next to her, Andrew tears open a condom wrapper, but the sound seems distant.

By the time she's rolled over onto her back, by the time Shane is on top of her, sliding her soaked, tangled panties down her thighs, his mouth gasping against her neck as he slides into her for the second time in twenty-four hours, she feels separated from the business of her extremities by the delicious, throbbing pleasure in her core.

And then she hears a second condom wrapper being torn open.

A second later, Shane halts in mid-thrust, still buried inside of her as his entire body goes rigid, as his breaths turn into a series of hissing gasps through clenched teeth. Cassidy reaches up to find her husband's chest coming to rest against Shane's upper back. She blinks, sees Andrew's face above her now as well, sees him tenderly kissing the nape of Shane's neck. Her hands travel from Shane's shoulders to her husband's shoulders directly above.

"Oh, fuck," Shane whispers, desperately, pain rippling through his words. "Oh, fuck." But laced through his pain are the sounds of hunger, need, and endurance. Still, Cassidy is afraid, afraid this is too much. She knows he rarely bottoms, has spent most of his adult life wondering if he doesn't have it in him or if he's never met the man powerful enough to flip him.

"Breathe," she whispers, taking his face in her hands. She would call the whole thing off right there if Shane wasn't still rock hard inside of her, motionless and rigid under Andrew's slow but determined invasion, but still hard, still throbbing inside of the condom.

"Breathe, Shane," she whispers. "Just breathe."

Shane winces, tears sprouting from his eyes. She can't tell if they're tears of pain or exertion, but they're *tears*, goddammit, so does it really matter? This was too far, too fast, and she has to end it now before everything flies off the rails.

"Shane, do you want us to stop?"

"No," he growls. "*Never*. Never stop." She feels him drawing back from inside of her, realizes this means he's sliding back onto Andrew's cock. "Belong to you…"

In her head, she finishes for him the words they whispered to each other the night before, when it seemed that shimmering spirits still hovered right outside the bedroom door. *Both of you. Always.* But Shane doesn't finish reciting these vows. His heaving breaths steal the power of speech from his lips, as he slowly, carefully rocks between her clutching heat and Andrew's overpowering penetration. His shuddering body searches out a never-before-felt rhythm, a composition unique to their three bodies, brought together in this way for the first time.

Shane's facial expressions are a wild parade of pain, pleasure, and abandon. But Andrew is pure determination, his arms wrapped around Shane's chest, devouring Shane's neck. She wants desperately to coax Shane past his final wall of resistance. But she knows she doesn't have this power. Not by herself anyway. Together, she and Andrew might be capable of it. But there are no words, no promises they can give Shane that will force him to surrender.

Shane has to choose. Shane has to give himself over to the dual embrace of Cassidy's wet heat and Andrew's unyielding force.

Please, Shane. Please. Give yourself to us. Belong to us.

It's silly to think he's read her mind, but that's exactly what she thinks when she feels the rhythm of Shane's thrusts increase. That's exactly what she thinks when she hears her husband's grunts and realizes Shane's ass now grips Andrew's cock with as much hunger and force as her folds grip Shane.

Cassidy screams with release, her hands clawing Shane's back. And then Shane's cry joins hers as he collapses against her, shuddering with another emotion as she feels him empty into the condom inside of her.

Breath returns to her lungs. Andrew lifts himself off of Shane and rolls over onto his side.

Shane continues to sob. When Cassidy opens her mouth to comfort him, Andrew brings one finger gently to her lips, silencing her.

"Give him a minute," Andrew whispers. "Give him a minute to realize he's ours now, then he'll be okay."

She wants to believe him, but she's terrified Shane's tears signal the end of this, that without Bastian Drake's magic, they'll once again be slaves to fear. Shane lifts his head from her chest. Her heart is racing. She's already visualizing him leaping off her and running from the house, from the full, world-changing implications of what they've done together now. Twice.

Andrew reaches up, cups the side of Shane's face in one hand. Surely, Shane can sense Cassidy's fear, knows full well the look that comes into her eyes when she's gripped by anticipation and dread. Surely, she has the look in her eyes right now.

Shane's eyes meet her own. He brings one of her hands to his mouth, kissing the tips of her fingers gently.

"Belong to you," Shane whispers.

"Both of you," Andrew whispers.

Cassidy's heart slows to a steady beat as Shane settles into her embrace. The words Bastian Drake's candle drew from them have once again rolled off their tongues. But the candle has been out for hours, its spirits and their sparkling residue nowhere in sight. It's just the three of them, their passion, their bravery. And now these words feel like vows.

Not all the words, she realizes. She's yet to add her final line to these, their new vows.

"Always," Cassidy whispers.

* * * *

Also from 1001 Dark Nights and Christopher Rice, discover Dance of Desire, The Surrender Gate, Kiss the Flame, and Desire & Ice.

Sign up for the 1001 Dark Nights Newsletter
and be entered to win a Tiffany Key necklace.

There's a new contest every month!

Go to www.1001DarkNights.com to subscribe.

As a bonus, all subscribers can download
FIVE FREE exclusive books!

Turn the page for a full list of the
1001 Dark Nights fabulous novellas...

Discover 1001 Dark Nights Collection Eight

Go to www.1001DarkNights.com for more information.

DRAGON REVEALED by Donna Grant
A Dragon Kings Novella

CAPTURED IN INK by Carrie Ann Ryan
A Montgomery Ink: Boulder Novella

SECURING JANE by Susan Stoker
A SEAL of Protection: Legacy Series Novella

WILD WIND by Kristen Ashley
A Chaos Novella

DARE TO TEASE by Carly Phillips
A Dare Nation Novella

VAMPIRE by Rebecca Zanetti
A Dark Protectors/Rebels Novella

MAFIA KING by Rachel Van Dyken
A Mafia Royals Novella

THE GRAVEDIGGER'S SON by Darynda Jones
A Charley Davidson Novella

FINALE by Skye Warren
A North Security Novella

MEMORIES OF YOU by J. Kenner
A Stark Securities Novella

SLAYED BY DARKNESS by Alexandra Ivy
A Guardians of Eternity Novella

TREASURED by Lexi Blake
A Masters and Mercenaries Novella

THE DAREDEVIL by Dylan Allen
A Rivers Wilde Novella

BOND OF DESTINY by Larissa Ione
A Demonica Novella

THE CLOSE-UP by Kennedy Ryan
A Hollywood Renaissance Novella

MORE THAN POSSESS YOU by Shayla Black
A More Than Words Novella

HAUNTED HOUSE by Heather Graham
A Krewe of Hunters Novella

MAN FOR ME by Laurelin Paige
A Man In Charge Novella

THE RHYTHM METHOD by Kylie Scott
A Stage Dive Novella

JONAH BENNETT by Tijan
A Bennett Mafia Novella

CHANGE WITH ME by Kristen Proby
A With Me In Seattle Novella

THE DARKEST DESTINY by Gena Showalter
A Lords of the Underworld Novella

Also from Blue Box Press

THE LAST TIARA by M.J. Rose

THE CROWN OF GILDED BONES by Jennifer L. Armentrout
A Blood and Ash Novel

THE MISSING SISTER by Lucinda Riley

Discover 1001 Dark Nights

Go to www.1001DarkNights.com for more information.

COLLECTION ONE

FOREVER WICKED by Shayla Black ~ CRIMSON TWILIGHT by Heather Graham ~ CAPTURED IN SURRENDER by Liliana Hart ~ SILENT BITE: A SCANGUARDS WEDDING by Tina Folsom ~ DUNGEON GAMES by Lexi Blake ~ AZAGOTH by Larissa Ione ~ NEED YOU NOW by Lisa Renee Jones ~ SHOW ME, BABY by Cherise Sinclair~ ROPED IN by Lorelei James ~ TEMPTED BY MIDNIGHT by Lara Adrian ~ THE FLAME by Christopher Rice ~ CARESS OF DARKNESS by Julie Kenner

COLLECTION TWO

WICKED WOLF by Carrie Ann Ryan ~ WHEN IRISH EYES ARE HAUNTING by Heather Graham ~ EASY WITH YOU by Kristen Proby ~ MASTER OF FREEDOM by Cherise Sinclair ~ CARESS OF PLEASURE by Julie Kenner ~ ADORED by Lexi Blake ~ HADES by Larissa Ione ~ RAVAGED by Elisabeth Naughton ~ DREAM OF YOU by Jennifer L. Armentrout ~ STRIPPED DOWN by Lorelei James ~ RAGE/KILLIAN by Alexandra Ivy/Laura Wright ~ DRAGON KING by Donna Grant ~ PURE WICKED by Shayla Black ~ HARD AS STEEL by Laura Kaye ~ STROKE OF MIDNIGHT by Lara Adrian ~ ALL HALLOWS EVE by Heather Graham ~ KISS THE FLAME by Christopher Rice~ DARING HER LOVE by Melissa Foster ~ TEASED by Rebecca Zanetti ~ THE PROMISE OF SURRENDER by Liliana Hart

COLLECTION THREE

HIDDEN INK by Carrie Ann Ryan ~ BLOOD ON THE BAYOU by Heather Graham ~ SEARCHING FOR MINE by Jennifer Probst ~ DANCE OF DESIRE by Christopher Rice ~ ROUGH RHYTHM by Tessa Bailey ~ DEVOTED by Lexi Blake ~ Z by Larissa Ione ~ FALLING UNDER YOU by Laurelin Paige ~ EASY FOR KEEPS by Kristen Proby ~ UNCHAINED by Elisabeth Naughton ~ HARD TO SERVE by Laura Kaye ~ DRAGON FEVER by Donna Grant ~ KAYDEN/SIMON by Alexandra Ivy/Laura Wright ~ STRUNG UP by Lorelei James ~ MIDNIGHT UNTAMED by Lara Adrian ~

TRICKED by Rebecca Zanetti ~ DIRTY WICKED by Shayla Black ~
THE ONLY ONE by Lauren Blakely ~ SWEET SURRENDER by
Liliana Hart

COLLECTION FOUR
ROCK CHICK REAWAKENING by Kristen Ashley ~ ADORING
INK by Carrie Ann Ryan ~ SWEET RIVALRY by K. Bromberg ~
SHADE'S LADY by Joanna Wylde ~ RAZR by Larissa Ione ~
ARRANGED by Lexi Blake ~ TANGLED by Rebecca Zanetti ~
HOLD ME by J. Kenner ~ SOMEHOW, SOME WAY by Jennifer
Probst ~ TOO CLOSE TO CALL by Tessa Bailey ~ HUNTED by
Elisabeth Naughton ~ EYES ON YOU by Laura Kaye ~ BLADE by
Alexandra Ivy/Laura Wright ~ DRAGON BURN by Donna Grant ~
TRIPPED OUT by Lorelei James ~ STUD FINDER by Lauren Blakely
~ MIDNIGHT UNLEASHED by Lara Adrian ~ HALLOW BE THE
HAUNT by Heather Graham ~ DIRTY FILTHY FIX by Laurelin
Paige ~ THE BED MATE by Kendall Ryan ~ NIGHT GAMES by CD
Reiss ~ NO RESERVATIONS by Kristen Proby ~ DAWN OF
SURRENDER by Liliana Hart

COLLECTION FIVE
BLAZE ERUPTING by Rebecca Zanetti ~ ROUGH RIDE by Kristen
Ashley ~ HAWKYN by Larissa Ione ~ RIDE DIRTY by Laura Kaye ~
ROME'S CHANCE by Joanna Wylde ~ THE MARRIAGE
ARRANGEMENT by Jennifer Probst ~ SURRENDER by Elisabeth
Naughton ~ INKED NIGHTS by Carrie Ann Ryan ~ ENVY by
Rachel Van Dyken ~ PROTECTED by Lexi Blake ~ THE PRINCE by
Jennifer L. Armentrout ~ PLEASE ME by J. Kenner ~ WOUND
TIGHT by Lorelei James ~ STRONG by Kylie Scott ~ DRAGON
NIGHT by Donna Grant ~ TEMPTING BROOKE by Kristen Proby
~ HAUNTED BE THE HOLIDAYS by Heather Graham ~
CONTROL by K. Bromberg ~ HUNKY HEARTBREAKER by
Kendall Ryan ~ THE DARKEST CAPTIVE by Gena Showalter

COLLECTION SIX
DRAGON CLAIMED by Donna Grant ~ ASHES TO INK by Carrie
Ann Ryan ~ ENSNARED by Elisabeth Naughton ~ EVERMORE by
Corinne Michaels ~ VENGEANCE by Rebecca Zanetti ~ ELI'S
TRIUMPH by Joanna Wylde ~ CIPHER by Larissa Ione ~
RESCUING MACIE by Susan Stoker ~ ENCHANTED by Lexi Blake

~ TAKE THE BRIDE by Carly Phillips ~ INDULGE ME by J. Kenner ~ THE KING by Jennifer L. Armentrout ~ QUIET MAN by Kristen Ashley ~ ABANDON by Rachel Van Dyken ~ THE OPEN DOOR by Laurelin Paige ~ CLOSER by Kylie Scott ~ SOMETHING JUST LIKE THIS by Jennifer Probst ~ BLOOD NIGHT by Heather Graham ~ TWIST OF FATE by Jill Shalvis ~ MORE THAN PLEASURE YOU by Shayla Black ~ WONDER WITH ME by Kristen Proby ~ THE DARKEST ASSASSIN by Gena Showalter

COLLECTION SEVEN

THE BISHOP by Skye Warren ~ TAKEN WITH YOU by Carrie Ann Ryan ~ DRAGON LOST by Donna Grant ~ SEXY LOVE by Carly Phillips ~ PROVOKE by Rachel Van Dyken ~ RAFE by Sawyer Bennett ~ THE NAUGHTY PRINCESS by Claire Contreras ~ THE GRAVEYARD SHIFT by Darynda Jones ~ CHARMED by Lexi Blake ~ SACRIFICE OF DARKNESS by Alexandra Ivy ~ THE QUEEN by Jen Armentrout ~ BEGIN AGAIN by Jennifer Probst ~ VIXEN by Rebecca Zanetti ~ SLASH by Laurelin Paige ~ THE DEAD HEAT OF SUMMER by Heather Graham ~ WILD FIRE by Kristen Ashley ~ MORE THAN PROTECT YOU by Shayla Black ~ LOVE SONG by Kylie Scott ~ CHERISH ME by J. Kenner ~ SHINE WITH ME by Kristen Proby

Discover Blue Box Press

TAME ME by J. Kenner ~ TEMPT ME by J. Kenner ~ DAMIEN by J. Kenner ~ TEASE ME by J. Kenner ~ REAPER by Larissa Ione ~ THE SURRENDER GATE by Christopher Rice ~ SERVICING THE TARGET by Cherise Sinclair ~ THE LAKE OF LEARNING by Steve Berry and MJ Rose ~ THE MUSEUM OF MYSTERIES by Steve Berry and MJ Rose ~ TEASE ME by J. Kenner ~ FROM BLOOD AND ASH by Jennifer L. Armentrout ~ QUEEN MOVE by Kennedy Ryan ~ THE HOUSE OF LONG AGO by Steve Berry and MJ Rose ~ THE BUTTERFLY ROOM by Lucinda Riley ~ A KINGDOM OF FLESH AND FIRE by Jennifer L. Armentrout

Discover More Christopher Rice

Dance of Desire
By Christopher Rice

When Amber Watson walks in on her husband in the throes of extramarital passion with one of his employees, her comfortable, passion-free life is shattered in an instant. Worse, the fate of the successful country music bar that bears her family's name suddenly hangs in the balance. Her soon to be ex-husband is one of the bar's official owners; his mistress, one of its employees. Will her divorce destroy her late father's legacy?

Not if Amber's adopted brother Caleb has anything to do with it. The wandering cowboy has picked the perfect time for a homecoming. Better yet, he's determined to use his brains and his fists to put Amber's ex in his place and keep the family business intact. But Caleb's long absence has done nothing to dim the forbidden desire between him and the woman the State of Texas considers to be his sister.

Years ago, when they were just teenagers, Caleb and Amber shared a passionate first kiss beside a moonlit lake. But that same night, tragedy claimed the life of Caleb's parents and the handsome young man went from being a family friend to Amber's adopted brother. Has enough time passed for the two of them to throw off the roles Amber's father picked for them all those years ago? Will their desire for each other save the family business or put it in greater danger?

READER ADVISORY. DANCE OF DESIRE contains fantasies of dubious consent, acted on by consenting adults. Readers with sensitivities to those issues should be advised.

* * * *

The Surrender Gate: A Desire Exchange Novel
By Christopher Rice

Emily Blaine's life is about to change. Arthur Benoit, the kindly multimillionaire who has acted as her surrogate father for years, has just told her he's leaving her his entire estate, and he only has a few months to live. Soon Emily will go from being a restaurant manager with a useless English degree to the one of the richest and most powerful women in New Orleans. There's just one price. Arthur has written a letter to his estranged son Ryan he hopes will mend the rift between them, and he wants Emily to deliver the letter before it's too late. But finding Ryan won't be easy. He's been missing for years. He was recently linked to a mysterious organization called The Desire Exchange. But is The Desire Exchange just an urban legend? Or are the rumors true? Is it truly a secret club where the wealthy can live out their most private sexual fantasies?

It's a task Emily can't undertake alone. But there's only one man qualified to help her, her gorgeous and confident best friend, Jonathan Claiborne. She's suspected Jonathan of working as a high-priced escort for months now, and she's willing to bet that while giving pleasure to some of the most powerful men in New Orleans, Jonathan has uncovered some possible leads to The Desire Exchange—and to Ryan Benoit. But Emily's attempt to uncover Jonathan's secret life lands the two of them in hot water. Literally. In order to escape the clutches of one of Jonathan's most powerful and dangerous clients, they're forced to act on long buried desires—for each other.

When Emily's mission turns into an undercover operation, Jonathan insists on going with her. He also insists they continue to explore their impossible, reckless passion for each other. Enter Marcus Dylan, the hard-charging ex-Navy SEAL Arthur has hired to keep Emily safe. But Marcus has been hired for another reason. He, too, has a burning passion for Emily, a passion that might keep Emily from being distracted and confused by a best friend who claims he might be able to go straight just for her. But Marcus is as rough and controlling as Jonathan is sensual and reckless. As Emily searches for a place where the rich turn their fantasies into reality, she will be forced to decide which one of her own long-ignored fantasies should become her reality. But as Emily, Jonathan, and Marcus draw closer to The Desire Exchange itself, they find their destination isn't just shrouded in mystery, but in magic as well.

* * * *

Kiss The Flame: A Desire Exchange Novella
By Christopher Rice

Are some risks worth taking?

Laney Foley is the first woman from her hard working family to attend college. That's why she can't act on her powerful attraction to one of the gorgeous teaching assistants in her Introduction to Art History course. Getting involved with a man who has control over her final grade is just too risky. But ever since he first laid eyes on her, Michael Brouchard seems to think about little else but the two of them together. And it's become harder for Laney to ignore his intelligence and his charm.

During a walk through the French Quarter, an intoxicating scent that reminds Laney of her not-so-secret admirer draws her into an elegant scented candle shop. The shop's charming and mysterious owner seems to have stepped out of another time, and he offers Laney a gift that could break down the walls of her fear in a way that can only be described as magic. But will she accept it?

Light this flame at the scene of your greatest passion and all your desires will be yours...

Lilliane Williams is a radiant, a supernatural being with the power to make your deepest sexual fantasy take shape around you with just a gentle press of her lips to yours. But her gifts came at a price. Decades ago, she set foot inside what she thought was an ordinary scented candle shop in the French Quarter. When she resisted the magical gift offered to her inside, Lilliane was endowed with eternal youth and startling supernatural powers, but the ability to experience and receive romantic love was removed from her forever. When Lilliane meets a young woman who seems poised to make the same mistake she did years before, she becomes determined to stop her, but that will mean revealing her truth to a stranger. Will Lilliane's story provide Laney with the courage she needs to open her heart to the kind of true love only magic can reveal?

* * * *

Desire & Ice: A MacKenzie Family Novella
by Christopher Rice

Danny Patterson isn't a teenager anymore. He's the newest and youngest sheriff's deputy in Surrender, Montana. A chance encounter with his former schoolteacher on the eve of the biggest snowstorm to hit Surrender in years shows him that some schoolboy crushes never fade. Sometimes they mature into grown-up desire.

It's been years since Eliza Brightwell set foot in Surrender. So why is she back now? And why does she seem like she's running from something? To solve this mystery, Danny disobeys a direct order from Sheriff Cooper MacKenzie and sets out into a fierce blizzard, where his courage and his desire might be the only things capable of saving Eliza from a dark force out of her own past.

About Christopher Rice

By the age of 30, Christopher Rice had published four New York Times bestselling thrillers, received a Lambda Literary Award and been declared one of People Magazine's Sexiest Men Alive. His first work of supernatural suspense, THE HEAVENS RISE, was a finalist for the Bram Stoker Award. His debut, A DENSITY OF SOULS, was published when the author was just 22 years old. A controversial and overnight bestseller, it was greeted with a landslide of media attention, much of it devoted to the fact that Christopher is the son of vampire chronicler, Anne Rice. Bestselling thriller writer (and Jack Reacher creator) Lee Child hailed Christopher's novel LIGHT BEFORE DAY as a "book of the year". Together with his best friend, New York Times bestselling novelist Eric Shaw Quinn, Christopher launched his own Internet radio show. THE DINNER PARTY SHOW WITH CHRISTOPHER RICE & ERIC SHAW QUINN is always playing at TheDinnerPartyShow.com and every episode is available for free download from the site's show archive or on iTunes. 47North, the science fiction, fantasy and horror imprint of Amazon Publishing, recently published his most recent supernatural thriller, THE VINES. And on December 9th, Thomas & Mercer, the crime and thriller imprint of Amazon Publishing, will release new editions of his previous bestsellers A DENSITY OF SOULS, THE SNOW GARDEN and LIGHT BEFORE DAY. He will continue the world of Thee Desire Exchange with a new erotic romance, THE SURRENDER GATE, due out from Evil Eye Concepts in early 2015.

The Surrender Gate
A Desire Exchange Novella
By Christopher Rice

"Arthur has a son who ran away from home years ago, when he was twenty," Emily says. "His name is Ryan. Ryan Benoit. Arthur's written him a letter and he wants me to find him and give it to him."

"As a condition of leaving you his fortune?" Dugas asks.

"It's not a condition. It's a request. And given that he's about to change my life forever, I'd say it's the very least I can do."

There is more bite in her tone than she'd intended, but Dugas seems more aroused by it than offended. "I see. Have you read this letter?" he asks.

"I have not. And I will not."

"Well, that *is* impressive. Certainly more self-control than you exhibited this evening. So you have no idea why Ryan ran away, but you're expected to find him and bring him back?"

"I'm expected to give him the letter. The letter is supposed to bring him back. At least that's what Arthur's hoping for."

"And Arthur has made no attempt to find his son before now?"

"No. I mean, yes. He has, but…"

"But *what?*" Jonathan asks.

"Ryan ran away so long ago that every few years Arthur has an age progression done on computer. Then he hires a private detective to go look for him. A few years ago, one of the detectives turned up what looked like a real lead. But at the time, Arthur didn't want to pursue it. Now that he's dying, he's had a change of heart."

"And the lead was?" Dugas asks.

"The P.I. said a man matching the latest progression was involved with some sort of secret *organization* called The Desire Exchange." Emily watches Jonathan to gauge his reaction to these words. He's nowhere near as startled as she'd hoped he'd be. "I've only heard that name one other time and it was from you. You just sort of mentioned it in passing so I thought—"

"You thought what?" Jonathan asks sharply. "That I was a member of a secret sex cult?"

"I just thought you might know more about it than you were letting on. But you wouldn't tell me unless—"

"—unless you caught me with a client and *embarrassed* it out of me?"

"Children," Dugas says. "Please."

"Emily. *Come on!* Some secret organization that helps millionaires live out their deepest sexual fantasies? It was somebody's idea of a joke. I thought it was funny. That's why I told you. It's not real, for Christ's sake."

"It is not a joke," George Dugas says quietly. His finality silences them both

The man seems incapacitated all of a sudden. By shock? Memories? Emily can't tell. If she hadn't looked to Jonathan so quickly when she'd said those three shiver-inducing words, she might have picked up on the older man's reaction before now.

"And it's *very* real," Dugas whispers.

He rises to his feet, takes his drink in hand, and strolls to the edge of the pool; as if it's wavering blue surface were a window onto the past. "The latest age progression. Describe it to me."

"He was about six feet tall when he ran away, so he should be around that now. Dirty blonde hair."

"Leave out the things he could have easily changed," Dugas says.

"Okay. Bright eyes that have a kind of slant to them that looks almost Eastern European. I guess they'd make him look kind of angry. Or amused, I'm not sure. Anyway, his facial features, they're all proportional, is what I'm trying to say. Especially his nose. He doesn't have one of those big Roman noses that can dominate a guy's face. Everything about him is more classic and all-American."

"Any birthmarks?" Dugas asks.

"Yes. A small strawberry-colored mark above his left collarbone."

This concise description causes Dugas to straighten and suck in a deep breath, as if a wave of pleasure is coursing through his entire body.

"Oh my," Dugas whispers. Then he takes a quick sip of his drink. "Oh, mymy*my*."

Jonathan breaks the silence. "Mr. Dugas, are you a *member* of The Desire Exchange?"

"The Desire Exchange doesn't have members. It's not a club. It's an *experience*."

"An experience you've apparently had," Emily says.

The older man drains the last of his cocktail with several long swallows. The mint sprig catches on the remaining ice cubes as he drinks.

Whatever it is, George Dugas has trouble remembering The Desire Exchange without the balm of whiskey and powdered sugar to soothe the hot fires of his lust.

"Have you *seen* Ryan Benoit?" Emily asks.

"How about I give you the chance to see him for yourself?" Dugas says. "For a price, of course. *Several* prices."

When Dugas starts for Emily's chair, Jonathan straightens, watching the man's every move.

"There's the price of admission, of course. That you will pay directly to the Exchange. After I've given you a reference. And make no mistake, you *must* have a reference. The admission…well, I'm sure Arthur Benoit will cover that for you. But he'll also need to give you some sort of fake identity, something that will make you appear to be in line with their usual clientele. Do you think he's up to it?"

Dugas is standing behind her chair now. Jonathan watches the man with the intensity of a cat watching a bird through a window. Emily studies Jonathan's facial expression with the same focus.

"Arthur would do anything to get Ryan that letter," Emily says. "Short of *hurting* people."

"No," Dugas whispers, hands coming to rest on her shoulders. "Of course not. Pain is not on the menu."

"And the price for your reference?" she asks.

Gently, he pulls open the flaps of her robe, exposing her breasts to the humid air. Her eyes flutter shut against her will as she braces for the feel of the man's hands on her flesh. But the feeling doesn't come. He continues to tug on the robe instead until the loose knot in the tie comes undone. Suddenly her thighs are exposed, and then her sex.

Jonathan gazes into her eyes, trying to read her every emotion, ready to spring into action as soon as she gives him the word, she's sure of it. But her head is swimming and there is heat traveling up her sternum. Rather than feeling violated, being gradually exposed this way makes her feel included in a delicious secret.

"The Desire Exchange isn't just about *your* fantasy," Dugas continues. "It's about surrendering to the fantasies of others as well. To do that, you have to let go of labels, of limits. Of fears."

"I'm still waiting to hear your price, Mr. Dugas."

The older man chuckles. "As if you'd ever say no, Miss Blaine. You'd be risking your incredible inheritance if you did."

"I'm risking my incredible inheritance by agreeing to find the only rightful heir. Some of us are motivated by other things than money, *sir*."

"Yes," Dugas says. With one final tug he has separated the flaps of the robe and draws it down over her back, rendering her fully nude and exposed. "Desire."

Jonathan is on the edge of his seat, nostrils flaring, rock-hard pecs rising and falling with his deep breaths. The head of his olive-skinned cock has emerged from the waistband of his briefs, glistening with his arousal. She tells herself it's just Dugas acting the part of the masculine aggressor that has Jonathan engorged. It can't be *her*, for Christ's sake. How many times has he seen her breasts before now? But she's right and she's wrong at the same time. It's not just her. And it's not just George Dugas. It's all of it. All three of them, the setting, the hint of danger, and the act of pure will that brought her here. It's this sudden swirl of desire they've been swept up by, and Emily realizes it's about to render comforting labels irrelevant.

"Nobody does anything for just one reason," Dugas whispers in her ear. "You can pretend you climbed onto my roof because you were after information that will help you find this Ryan Benoit. But you'd be lying. You'd be lying if you didn't also admit you wanted to see the expression on your best friend's face while he was in the throes of passion with a strange man."

On behalf of 1001 Dark Nights,

Liz Berry, M.J. Rose, and Jillian Stein would like to thank ~

Steve Berry
Doug Scofield
Benjamin Stein
Kim Guidroz
InkSlinger PR
Dan Slater
Asha Hossain
Chris Graham
Chelle Olson
Kasi Alexander
Jessica Johns
Dylan Stockton
Richard Blake
and Simon Lipskar

Made in the USA
Monee, IL
18 April 2021

64941323R00069